Eleanor Kirk

Up Broadway and its sequel

A life story

Eleanor Kirk

Up Broadway and its sequel
A life story

ISBN/EAN: 9783337141141

Printed in Europe, USA, Canada, Australia, Japan

Cover: Foto ©Raphael Reischuk / pixelio.de

More available books at **www.hansebooks.com**

UP BROADWAY,

AND ITS SEQUEL.

A Life Story.

BY ELEANOR KIRK.

[NELLIE AMES.]

NEW YORK:

Carleton, Publisher, Madison Square.

LONDON: S. LOW, SON, & CO.

MDCCCLXX.

Stereotyped at
THE WOMEN'S PRINTING HOUSE,
Eighth Street and Avenue A,
New York.

*"THE TRUTH, THE WHOLE TRUTH, AND
NOTHING BUT THE TRUTH."*

UP BROADWAY.

CHAPTER I.

NO naturally kind-hearted and benevolent person can—even after years' experience with the beggars, grinders and sweepers who crowd the streets of New York—become sufficiently inured to destitution and misery to pass, without notice, their pitiful faces and outstretched hands. Now I, in common with many others, have been acquainted with these appeals for several years, and have not, after continued and systematic fleecing, become so hardened—or so sensible—that my heart does not ache an hour after, when I have—from inability to afford relief, or from a determination to bestow my mite where

I am sure it will be well used and appreciated—passed without notice.

In a walk from Pearl to Eighth, the other day—or rather in a contemplated walk, for I did not complete it on that occasion—I decided to speak to every beggar who accosted me, and discover, if possible, what especial phase of poverty was represented by each. Not that my pocket was especially long at that time, or my *porte monnaie* unusually full, not at all; but some information might be gained by such a process that could not be obtained in any other manner; and then, if my search was rewarded by really worthy objects, I could, by the assistance of charitable friends, see that they were provided for. I thought to walk a block without being accosted; but, on the steps of the Central National Bank sat a little woe-begone bundle of rags, which upon rising and advancing toward me, I found to be of the feminine gender. My weakness has always been for this description of sufferers, and, consequently, there was no lack of sympathy.

" Well, my dear, what do you want?" I asked kindly of the little one, whose eyes shone out as bright as stars on a frosty night from the mass of curly, unkempt hair which surrounded a face made prematurely old by this conflict with sin and poverty.

"Don't *dear* me," said she, almost fiercely. "I got enough of that at the Mission. '*Dear* child,' '*good* child,' 'trust in the Lord, child,' with a bundle of tracts, and no dinner," she continued, ironically.

"Where do you live, my child?" I asked—this time careful of my adjectives.

"I ain't your child, nor nobody's child, nor God's child; and I hadn't anything to do with being made, no more than that old horse had; and nobody need tell me that there is a good Father who loves his children; 'tain't no such thing. Do you suppose, if I was the Lord, I'd starve poor folks to death that I made myself?" and the eager eyes looked into my face, the desire to reconcile apparent incongruities being stronger, for the moment, than her desire for good. Here was a poser. How could I talk to the suffering child of faith? How could I tell her that God loveth whom he chasteneth, and that the more she endured, the greater was God's care and affection for her?   So I simply said:

"Such things have troubled me a great deal; but I cannot explain to you, here, what I do think on these subjects.   You are suffering; you are hungry and cold; now tell me about yourself. Perhaps I can do you some good.   Have you a father living?"

"No!" and the eyes took on a wondering look. "I don't think I ever had a father."

"And your mother?"

"Oh, I've got one of them; but she's no good."

"No *good*," said I; "what do you mean?" and I tried to put a little sternness into my voice and manner; but she took no notice.

"She stays out all night, and sleeps and cries all day; sometimes she brings home something to eat, and more times the doesn't; but I tell you"— and now her eyes flashed fire —"she never forgets to bring something to drink."

"Where do you live?"

"Round here in Mulberry street."

"Will you take me to your mother?"

"What, with those good clothes on?   I guess

not?" And the strange child laughed merrily as she glanced at my plain street-dress, which was to her purple and fine linen. Upon assuring her that I was not at all afraid, she led the way to her miserable home.

"There she is," said the little girl, pointing to a figure lying on a bundle of straw in the corner.

"Mother, here is a lady come to see you; wake up a minute;" accompanying her words with a brisk shaking.

"A lady!" and the figure, by no means as inanimate as it appeared, arose and confronted me. Such a pair of coal-black eyes, and such a pallid face, I never saw in my life before. No tigress ever looked fiercer—and no woman more beautiful when she discovered I had come in all friendliness to be of service, if possible.

"Don't be angry, mamma," said the girl; "the lady hasn't got a single *tract*."

"This is no place for you, madam, and it is impossible for you to do me any good," was her greeting, in clear, ringing tones.

"Your little girl is very thinly clad," I ventured to remark, glancing significantly at some trumpery hanging round, which was evidently worn by the woman on her midnight rambles.

"Then you think the mother dresses better than the child?" she inquired, smiling disdainfully. "Those clothes get her all the bread she eats. Now I suppose you understand my profession."

"Perfectly," I replied, trying to repress all emotion. "And if you are satisfied with that profession, I have no more to say. But your little girl?"

"Ah, you would like to take her away, I suppose; get her a place at service, maybe—is that your game? But you don't do it, madam," she interrupted, excitedly. "Perhaps you think I don't love her—perhaps I don't; but you just try to wrench her away from me, and then see. Mary, come here."

"I am not afraid of this lady, mother. I would like to go with her. I don't like to stay here all alone nights with rats and mice, and then have you drink out of that bottle all day. Oh, Mrs.! if you would only get me a suit of boy's clothes somewhere! I could earn lots of money. I'd black gentlemen's boots and nobody'd know ; but I can't do anything with these duds. However came I to be a nasty, good-for-nothing girl, mother ? I tell you, Mrs., boys can do a heap ! "

I looked from that child to the parent, noted the same broad foreheads, and intellectual countenances, and wondered if any influence could reclaim the mother and preserve the child.

"I do not wish to be impertinent, and pry into affairs which are none of my concern," I ventured, at last, "but I am interested in your history. Won't you please tell me something of yourself, and how you came here, for I perceive you have not always lived in this squalid style."

She hesitated a moment. Then, offering me her only stool, said :

"I will, and will tell the truth, too. Sit down."

CHAPTER II.

A STRANGE kind of smile illumined the wan features for a moment as she looked into my face, which must have expressed every shade of feeling from that which the countenance of our blessed Saviour indicated to that of shrinking and terror, as the dreadful squalidness of the place, and my apparently unprotected condition, came home to me.

"You are not used to such scenes as these," she said. "Do not be in the least alarmed: you are just as safe in this tumble-down old shanty in Five Points as you would be in many places on aristocratic, stylish Fifth avenue. According to my views, there isn't much difference in the crime committed in the two places. Women there have their paramours and affinities. The man next door courts his neighbor's wife while the other fellow trips the light fantastic with still another man's property. Children are conceived, some of them legitimately, but children are troublesome comforts, and no fashionable woman wishes to be bothered with an increasing family! So Dr. So-and-so, who lives in close contiguity, and most sumptuously, is called. The result — an abortion; and the murderer pockets his big fee, and keeps on his work of destruction. These babies will all confront their unnatural mothers one of these days in the other country — and, madam," clutching my arm with the grip of a mad woman, "I'd rather be Mary Montgomery then than one of these. What do *you* say ?"

"There is no mistake, my dear," said I, endeavoring to be calm, "that infanticide is one of the most terrible and glaring evils possible to conceive of ; but the scandalous behavior of women in high life does not remove one iota of your sin or mine, or make it any less in the sight of God."

"That's so," she continued thoughtfully. "But some way it eases one's soul occasionally to make such comparisons. Think of it as you may, it *is* a relief, when Mrs. Gen. —— or Capt. —— passes one like me, drawing away her skirt as she does so, as if the slightest touch were contamination, to think, madam, your stock won't be worth as much as mine in the great by-and-by."

The woman stopped a moment, closed her eyes, as if to shut out some crushing memories, and the little bundle of rags—the child—with the sweet and wonderfully intelligent face, crept close to my side.

"Say, Mrs.," said she softly, "please to tell me what these things are for," pointing with her little red finger to the miserable surroundings.

"What things?" I asked, while the bunch in my throat grew bigger and tears filled my eyes.

"Why is all this badness? and this dreadful cold room? and these rags, and mother's headaches and **crying?** I don't like 'em; they don't agree with me; and I can't bear these clothes. I never was clean and nice; and what is it all for? Why mayn't I have good things, and why mayn't mother stop staying out nights, and drinking out of that black bottle? *I* never did nothing to nobody; what does God punish *me* for?"

I have been nonplussed many a time with the questions of my own little ones, but never was my theology so thoroughly squelched before; and I only answered, "My poor child! I do not wonder that you ask these questions; but I am utterly unable to give you any light."

How could I make that poor persecuted babe understand that God loveth whom he chasteneth? No, indeed. I didn't attempt it; for in the heaviest of my own afflictions, that and kindred passages failed to give me the least satisfaction. I make this statement with due reverence, for I honestly believe that God is at the helm, and will bring things out all right one of these days. But why the innocent should suffer for the guilty will take more light and grace than I ever expect to attain to in this world to either explain or reconcile.

"I want to tell you of myself," said the hollow-eyed woman, breaking in upon a solemn pause, and fondly stroking the little one's curls. "Now, Mary, you go and sit with old Mother Thurston while I talk to this lady."

The child obeyed—only saying as she went out—"Please call me before this lady goes; I want to see her again."

2

"My name is Mary Montgomery," she continued, looking into her lap. "I was born in Philadelphia, of American parents, and very respectable parents, too. They are both dead now, thank God. I was well brought up, well educated, and quite accomplished. These hands," holding up her attenuated fingers, "do not remind one very forcibly of Beethoven's sonatas, or Mozart's symphonies, yet they could manage them all once. I wonder if I could play a single tune now? My father and mother never seemed to love me — at least as I wanted to be loved. They were never demonstrative. My first impression of my mother was her iciness, and the extreme formality of my father in all matters of social intercourse. At seventeen I had never been in the society of young men at all. My father would not consent to an evening party, a dance, or to the least mingling with the terrible class of which he made one. One afternoon, returning from my aunt's, I strayed into Chestnut street and stole an hour's walk, as I had done many times before. As I stood looking into a book-store, I felt that some one stood beside me, and was conscious that a gentleman was examining my features attentively. I turned with the intention of saying something sharp and saucy — but his pleasant and respectful expression speedily drove that idea from my mind. Without the least reserve he said:

"'Here we have all the poets, and most dazzlingly arrayed too. Which of the number do you prefer?' enumerating the authors.

"It seemed very proper and natural for me to answer him. So after a little conversation concerning our favorites, he walked with me until within a block of my house, when I bade him good afternoon. During our conversation, I had given him my name and some idea of my life, and had promised to meet him the next day, in front of the book-store in Chestnut street. A few interviews, and the man had declared his love, and I had confessed mine. It would never do to mention this to my parents. I should have been immediately confined in my own room, with no prospect of ever seeing my lover again during the term of my natural life. So we continued to meet stealthily. At last, he proposed a secret marriage, saying that he would take me to New

York, and, after the ceremony was performed, we could plead for the forgiveness and blessing of my parents. I agreed to **that** also. Oh! I loved him so, that I would have sunk my soul in the lowest depths of the inferno to have given him pleasure! and oh, my God, how I love him this minute! how I love him! how I love him! Excuse me, these exhibitions are not interesting to you," and then continued. "I left my home one day with nothing save the clothes I had on. We took a train to New York—then a carriage from the depot to some minister's house and were married. After that to a hotel, where we remained for a few days, and then my husband took me home. Oh, and wasn't it home? Everything that money could buy was lavished upon that house; and as I crept into his arms, after a careful examination of every nook and corner, I thanked God from the bottom of my heart that I had found so good and loving a husband."

CHAPTER III.

"OH! my dear lady," she said, "there never was such happiness since the bliss Adam and Eve enjoyed in the garden of Eden as we experienced for more than a year. My husband often remained away from me all night, telling me that business compelled him; but he would invariably make it up by remaining by my side the greater portion of the succeeding day. I had no care, no responsibility. Life was love, and love was life. I ate it, drank it, feasted upon it, revelled in it. In short, I bowed down before my idol and worshipped him. One year passed, and my Mary was born, the little girl who brought you here."

"The child of honest wedlock, then?" I interrupted, and without thinking.

"Oh don't, madam—as I supposed; as I believed;" she replied distractedly. "But wait until I finish. Please don't anticipate, or I shall never have strength enough left to finish the sickening details. She was a darling baby and her father was so fond of her. I used sometimes to grow jealous of the caresses lavished upon her. I used to wonder why my husband never took me to parties, and why we never received company like other families in upper-tendom, and why he always chose the evenings to take me out for a walk or drive, and I would occasionally express to him my astonishment at the way our domestic programme was arranged. He always replied after this style: ' Is my little wife dissatisfied? If so, I will invite half New York to entertain her. It is because I love her so, that, buried in my own heart, I desire to satisfy her with what she finds there.'

"We read and sung, and sketched, and petted baby, with no cloud to disturb our serenity. By-and-by it came without a single gust of preparation. My husband generally returned to me about three in the afternoon. One day he was a little later than usual, and just as I was going down to the dining-room to see that everything was in order for dinner, I found that the servant was admitting visitors into the hall. This was so rare that I stopped to see who was coming.

"'Does Mrs. —— live here?'—mentioning my name—I heard a lady ask in low tones.

"'She does, madam; will you please walk into the parlor?' the servant replied.

"I drew back into the library and waited for her to enter. It might be my mother, I thought, to whom I had written for forgiveness several times, but never had received an answer. Imagine my surprise, when a lady, elegantly dressed, followed by a nurse carrying an infant, swept by into the drawing-room. I immediately passed in after them.

"'Mrs. ——, I suppose,' said the lady, with a look of unutterable scorn upon her handsome features.

"'Yes, madam,' I replied. 'Whom have I the honor of addressing?'

"'Not the least consequence, Mrs. —— ; I have business with your husband.'

"'I am expecting him in every moment,' I replied. 'Please make yourself comfortable.'

"Just then the nurse brought my babe to the door. She was then about six months old, just able to sit up alone. The other babe was apparently about the same age. I placed my darling on the carpet, and held out my hands to the other little one. She came to me in a moment, held up her cherry lips for a kiss, and I removed her cap and cloak, and placed her beside mine. Oh! merciful Father! they were as alike as two roses from the same stem. But even then I was unsuspicious.

"'How do you account, madam,' said the woman in tones cold and polished as glittering steel, 'for the remarkable resemblance between these two children?'

"They were both dressed in white, with blue sashes and sleeve trimmings. I did not at first reply, but laughingly removed my chain from my watch-guard, and slipped it around the neck of my Mary, saying, as I did so, 'I will place a mark on mine to distinguish her, else, I fear, we shall hardly be able to tell them apart.' Pretty soon I heard my husband's night-key, and in a

second his voice, singing the old Scotch ballad
(he always sang as he entered the house), —

> " 'Oh, Mary is my darling, my darling, my darling,
>   Oh! where in the world is my darling
>   That I do not find her here?'

" 'My husband has come,' said I. 'I will
bring him to you.'

" 'There is a lady in the parlor for you,' I
said, and flew to his embrace.

" 'A lady!' he repeated in a strange whisper. 'You are joking, dear,' but an awful pale-
ness overspread his face. 'Tell her I am not in;
that's a good little wife. How come she to be
admitted?' but before I could leave the hall, the
fury was upon him.

" 'Oh!' said she, calling him by his right name.
You see, my dear lady, I had never known it.
'Did you think to keep on deceiving me in this
style? Come here and look;' and clutching him
furiously by the arm, she almost dragged him into the parlor. The two babies began to crow and
laugh, clapping their tiny hands in their delight
at seeing him. Oh, my — wasn't that fearful!

and as he threw himself into a chair near them
in a perfect agony of despair, the little darlings,
determined that he should notice them, played
with his feet, and finally, failing to attract his
attention, commenced to cry piteously. I did
not then comprehend the depth of the dreadful
affair; and taking the infants from the carpet I
placed one on each knee of the man I had called
husband. He pressed them both to his bosom
for a moment, saying as he did so, 'Mary, you
have killed me.'

"'But what does all this mean?' I at last
found breath to ask.

"'It means, madam,' said the self-possessed
woman, 'that that man is my lawful husband,
and that child his legitimate offspring. It means
that you are his mistress, and that babe the child
of shame and lust.'

"'You are a liar,' said I, springing towards
her. 'Unsay those dreadful words, or these hands
will force an entrance to your black heart;' and
God only knows what else, in my insane agony, I
did say.

" ' Ask *him* if it is not so,' replied the woman, still cool and polished.

" 'Mary,' said my—my—oh, yes—my husband; let me call him that once more. ' Curse me if you will. I am utterly unworthy a single thought. That woman, proud, overbearing and cold, I never loved, but she is just what she represents herself, my lawful wife

" ' And I—I—I am what ? ' I shrieked.

" ' My darling,' he replied, 'my heart's choice! but in the eyes of a cruel world—just what she has told you ; my—mistress. I loved you, Mary; your beauty and your innocence dazzled me. My heart was hungry for you, and I foolishly thought I could provide for all without being detected, but that bloodhound has traced me, and we are betrayed. I am—oh, my—a miserable wretch.'

" 'But our marriage '—

" ' Was a farce. I was not man enough to attempt bigamy even.' "

CHAPTER IV.

HAT did I do?" she repeated, as under my breath, my heart beating in sympathy for the poor narrator, I could not help asking.

"Do! I snatched my babe from the floor, and, with just a few articles of wearing apparel and a small sum of money, I left the house without another word; left that cold, haughty woman still in the parlor; left the only person I loved on earth, except my little one. No one saw me go. I took the evening train for Philadelphia; went to my father's house at eleven o'clock at night; found that my mother had died a few weeks previous. My father came stiffly into the parlor; inquired what might be my business with him— to transact it as quickly as possible, as he was in a hurry to close the house and retire. I told him that I had brought my baby home to make a visit.

Oh, I did so hope to soften his heart! The little one clapped her tiny hands, laughed up into his iron face, called him papa! but he took no notice I then continued to ask him if he had one kind word for his daughter?

"'Not one,' he replied, flying into an ungovernable rage. 'Where is your keeper, madam, the father of that child?' he roared. 'If he be dead, I may, perhaps, for decency sake, tolerate you under my roof—but that brat, never. Say?' grasping my arm and shaking me fiercely—'yes or no! Is *he dead* or living?'

"'Living, father,' said I, 'and likely to live. I have come to you to-night for shelter. I have no other home. Do let me stay with you?'

"'When that child of disgrace and its damned parent are both in the grave, come to me, and I will feed and clothe you; but with those evidences of shame about you, never, never, never, so help me God!'

"Oh, how those memories madden me!" said the woman, rising from her seat on the floor and pacing rapidly up and down a moment or two. "Sometimes, madam," she continued, her whole

expression changing from the fierce, almost des-
pairing look her face had all the time worn to
one of weird and wonderful illumination; "sometimes, I hear my father's voice (he died, you see,
only a few months after this), saying, 'Mary!
Mary! my child, forgive me? I knew not what
I did. Upon my soul rests your downfall!' I
hear this voice in the night—hear it in the
day—hear it when on my Broadway beat! It
seeks me here, there, and everywhere! 'Forgive
me, child! Oh, forgive me!'

"And you have forgiven him," I ventured to
remark, through a blinding mist of tears.

"Have I?" she replied, pausing in her walks,
and looking me straight in the face with those
wondrous eyes of hers. "Have I? Perhaps *you*
know more about it than I do!"

Aye, there was rebellion there. Rebellion in
the curve of the lip, rebellion in the toss of the
head, beautiful, even now, bowed down though
it was with the weight of sin and shame.

"Forgive him! Who forgives me? When
Fifth avenue takes me by the hand; when ministers stop preaching of charity, and put some of

it into practice; when Christians remember that the only reprimand of Jesus to the fallen woman was 'Go, and sin no more,' then will I forgive the man who sent me and my baby to perdition. When do you suppose that will be? You can be gentle and kind to me, *here.* You dare let your tears fall now, that there is no one by to observe your weakness; but suppose sometimes returning from opera or lecture, acompanied by your friends, you should meet me, do you think you would have a kind word for me then? No, indeed. You would pity me, I know, because you are naturally loving and sympathetic, but to go contrary to society's requirements and conventionalisms, you would not *dare!* I'll tell you what I will do. I will leave Fifth avenue and the rest of the world to their own devices, and promise this, since you are so earnest in regard to my most unnatural parent: I will forgive when you, with your select few, unexpectedly meeting me, can say, 'Good evening, my friend; I am glad to see you.'"

"Then allow me to tell you," I replied, "that your father is forgiven, if forgiveness, which I certainly do not believe, can depend upon such contingencies for its evidences and expression. I should neither be ashamed nor afraid to speak to you, meet you under what circumstances I might. But I must certainly question your right to demand this. I sometimes fear that the passage of Scripture where Jesus commands the one without sin to cast the first stone, has, from its singular perversion, done more harm than good." Those fierce eyes glared down into my soul; but for the first time in my life I shrank not from giving pain. The surgeon probes deeply when he would discover the nature and depth of the wound he desires to heal, so I looked away for a moment from the glowing countenance and continued: "When Jesus forgave that erring woman, he said, 'Go, and sin no more.' There was never a word in regard to her continuing in the paths of immorality, or the duty of the public towards one guilty of such persistence. We are counselled, I admit, to a boundless charity; we are told to forgive seventy times seven; but after all that, the public sentiment which denies to those guilty of transgressing human and divine

laws the privileges of social life, is, in my estimation, a healthy one. Although I could and
would accost you kindly under any and all circumstances, yet you have no right to expect it,
unless you change the whole current of your life,
and dertermine to turn your back upon those
unholy influences forever."

I had said more than I intended, for it is never
best to preach much to these sufferers; but as I
continued, the fierce look fled from her eyes, and
she replied honestly:

"Well, I never thought of that before. To
tell the truth, I never associated Jesus' forgiveness with any idea of the cessation of sin."

Now this may appear very singular to readers,
that such construction should be placed by any
intelligent person upon so apparently lucid a
passage; but I am free to say, after an extended
observation, that nothing in the Bible has ever
been so grossly misconstrued and acted upon as
this.

"I scarcely know," said she musingly, "whether
I shall bless or curse the fate that sent you here
to-day. One or the other, I assure you. I had

3

tried so long to stop thinking, and had settled so many things to my satisfaction, now I shall be compelled to go all over the ground again. But, as I was saying," going back to her story again, "with my baby in my arms, at the hour of midnight, cold and dark, I walked out of my father's house, and heard him carefully bolt the door as I walked off the marble stoop. A servant who had lived in our family for years, with whom I was a great favorite, followed me from the back entrance, took my little one, and led me to her sister's house, where I was comfortably cared for until the next day, when I left for New York, determined to fight out the battle of life here— and I have."

CHAPTER V.

THE winter sun slanted into the comfort-less room, reminding me that the day was almost spent, and the better plan was to leave and come again the next afternoon. She saw my glance and interpreted it aright.

'Yes, you had better go now," said she, with a pained look. "Mary shall see you to Broadway; no one ever molests her."

"And now," said I, "please tell me what you have in the house for your supper. And if there is not some way of making a cheerful fire."

"I have money enough," she replied, "to procure everything we need to-night, and Mary will soon go to bed, so it will be of no use to make up any more fire."

"And shall you retire with your little daughter?" I required, looking her straight in the eye.

"Oh no!" she said, returning my glance unshrinkingly. "I have an engagement."

The reader can imagine my feelings. Pity, sympathy, a desire to take the poor tempest-tossed woman in my arms and fly with her to some spot out of the reach of temptation, filled my soul. My position was a delicate one. I realized of how much service would be a word fitly spoken; and if ever I prayed in my life, I prayed then that I might be given, not only the right spirit, but that which is often quite as essential, the right language in which to clothe this spirit of longing and sympathy. Many and many a person in their dealings with different classes of unfortunates, with as earnest a desire to be of service as ever burned in the soul of man or woman, have blundered fearfully in this respect, and, by some unlucky sentence, or apparently unfeeling interrogative have set impassable barriers between themselves and the objects of their interest. Providence spared me the necessity of assuming the initiative. As I stood wondering what it was best to say — in what manner I could reach that part of her nature I most desired to reach, she remarked pleasantly:

"Excuse me, madam, but I know what you are thinking about. I see it all in your eyes. You want me to promise that I will not go out to-night. Isn't that it?"

"Exactly," I replied, while that dreadful bunch in my throat grew (to coin a word) unswallowable.

"Well," she resumed, "I promise, upon my word and honor, if you can believe in either, after all I have told you, that I will not step foot into the street this night?"

There was a touching wistfulness in the tone which satisfied me that one victory had been achieved. I had won her *loving* confidence, and that under the circumstances seemed to me a wonderful stride in the right direction. Please, dear reader, do not think me foolishly egotistical in this little narrative. If I do not give you the particulars as they occurred (for this is no work of fiction), I shall not be able to make you thoroughly acquainted with my strange and fallen heroine.

"You will excuse me, I know," she continued, "for being so bold, but please remember that no human being has spoken a kind word to me since — since — *he* did;" and here the woman broke down entirely, and buried her face in her hands, sobbing bitterly. Oh tears, blessed tears! under such circumstances, a salvation. The fountains were opened, and she wept unrestrainedly.

"I thank you a thousand times for this first proof of your confidence," I ventured to say, striving to be calm. "I shall leave you now without fear, and will come again to-morrow about the same hour; and now please call your little girl." The little child came with a disappointed look on her care-worn face, but she brightened up when she found she was to accompany me away and that I had promised to return on the morrow.

"Mary," said I, as we reached the street, "your mother has promised not to go out to-night."

"What?" said she, clasping her little hands and coming to a dead halt. "Won't that be nice? I'll have a bully sleep to-night! I guess there is a God, and I just guess *He is* good sometimes There isn't anybody that feels good all the time, *is there ?*"

Upon questioning the little one as to eatables, fire, etc., I found that their living was principally bread and tea, and that the little gray-looking concern in the fireplace could be made to cook very nicely. "What would you like most to have for your supper, Mary, supposing you had the choice given you ?" I inquired.

"Oh, meat!" said she, "meat! I believe I could eat a whole cow."

"Well then, meat you shall have," I replied, giving the child some change. "Go home and make a good fire, and have a good supper, and more than all, little one, try to believe that although there are hosts of things which none of us can understand, yet, if we do the best we can, as near right as we can, that we shall some day obtain our reward."

"And you believe that ?" she queried, with a rare smile.

"From the bottom of my heart," I made answer.

"Then I will try to," she replied. "But

everything is so awful bad, and I'm so awful ragged and so awful dirty. I can't make that right, because I do like to look like other good folks, and have mother too; but never mind, I will wait for you here to-morrow;" and the little one, with a tight squeeze of my hand, ran quickly away, leaving me, wondering but thankful, once more on gay Broadway. Aye, friends, the wealth of the world could not purchase that day's experience. These words kept ringing in my ears, all the way home and the tune was a merry one—"There is more joy in heaven over one sinner that repenteth than over ninety and nine just persons that need no repentance," and somehow (of course it was all imagination, but wonderfully pleasant) the faces of my dear, departed mother and father looked smilingly out of every cloud; and a sweet voice seemed to whisper, "Inasmuch as ye do it unto one of the least of these," and what, in the world's estimation, could be of less consequence than an abandoned woman?

The next afternoon, at the appointed time, I met the little girl at the same place. The child's hair was nicely combed, and her hands and face as clean as soap and water could make them.

"How is your mother?" I asked.

"Well, I dunno?" she answered. "She cried dreadful hard, seems to me, most all night, but she looks real nice this afternoon."

Sure enough, the room was nicely swept, a bright fire burned in the little stove, and the bundle of straw which answered for a bed was covered with an old quilt and tidily arranged.

"How pleasant this seems," I remarked, noticing that two chairs had been added to the furniture. "Now, I am going to take off my things and you will begin where you left off yesterday, and then we can put our heads together and see what we had best do." My new friend peered into my face curiously, but I chatted gaily, only wishing to convey the *shadow* of an idea that I intended to bring about a revolution in her affairs. Mary was dispatched, this time very much against her will, to Mother Thurston, but some warm stockings and underclothes, with a dress or two and a brush and comb, which I had collected from friends, did the work, and the child left, laughing and crying hysterically.

"As I was telling you," the woman continued, "I returned to New York. I spent one whole week hunting for work. Every place I went I was compelled to carry my baby. All looked at me suspiciously. Finally, in despair, I went where shirts and men's underclothing were given out, found an old woman who took care of Mary, and promised to board us for three dollars a week. The first work I carried home I was confronted by the proprietor, who, after asking me several questions about myself, ended by informing me that he would give me a better quality of work, better pay, and all that sort of thing. He did so, and I found myself able to earn from six to eight dollars a week. He seemed very kind, and I believed, notwithstanding my wretched experience, that he was my friend. One evening I was surprised by a visit from the man, who informed me that it was his practice to call occasionally on his employés. I swallowed that also, without the least suspicion."

CHAPTER VI

YOU can understand, madam," continued the heart-broken woman, "how very easy it was for me to be imposed upon. The descent from affluence had been so sudden that I could not realize the poverty and disgrace it had entailed upon me. I had been guilty of no sin except that of leaving my parents for the man I loved; and it took a good many hard knocks to enable me to comprehend that a woman toiling every day for her bread and butter was not a fit candidate for respectable society. So when Mr. —— called upon me in a friendly manner, stating that ever since he had been in business he had made it a practice to call occasionally on his employés, how could I be expected to look through the crust of deceit and treachery that enveloped the man, and read the depravity hidden away in his black soul! He represented

himself as a Christian, too; invited me to go to a
Methodist conference meeting, desired to know
if I had ever been converted, and if I considered
my calling and election sure, etc. On one occasion he prayed with me most earnestly. This
state of things continued several weeks, during
which time I made excellent wages, and got on
comfortably. But Heaven only knows how unhappy I was. One evening the old woman I
boarded with was away to church, and my employer called. I had never before been a
moment alone with him. Something, I scarcely
knew what, had always kept me from lighting
him to the door, although he had once or twice
especially requested it. This evening I had cried
until, fearful of spoiling my work, I laid it away;
and when I recognized his knock upon the door, a
peculiar warning, or premonition of evil, caused
the cold perspiration to stand in great beads
upon my face. His greeting was polite and
unexceptionable. I became in a measure assured. He rallied me upon my swollen eyes,
reasoned with me in regard to the utter useless-
ness and folly of tears, assured me that I should

always have a friend in him, and ended by drawing his chair closer to mine, and inquiring in low tones if I had not seen, from the very commencement, that his feelings toward me were not the ordinary feelings of friendship, but a deeper, truer, more passionate yearning than this word could ever suggest? I started back in horror. Then light commenced to dawn.

"' Do not be afraid of me, Mary,' he urged in the low, hissing tones of a serpent. 'You shall never take another stitch—never do another day's work; you shall be mine to care for—mine to keep ; you shall have your own earnings, and be mistress of your own establishment, and baby shall be to me as my own child.'

"'Have I not heard you, Mr. —— speak of your wife on several occasions?' I inquired, with as much calmness as I could assume.

"'Why, of course you have, you little simpleton; but didn't you know that it is all the fashion for men and their wives to hate each other cordially, and seek each their own pleasure in their own peculiar way? If you don't, let me enlighten you. My wife does just as she pleases. I never question, and *vice versa.* I loved you, Mary, as soon as I saw you. Now tell me that you will allow me to remove you from this horrible place to-morrow.'

"I looked at myself in the old woman's quaint little mirror, and wondered that I didn't fall dead at the man's feet. There I stood, the heart-broken victim of one wealthy New York merchant, dishonored and disgraced; and now, before the iron in my soul had had time to cool in the least, another of the same profession makes similar overtures. Aye, but I loved the first— how well Omniscience only knows. Whether I should, had I discovered his treachery before our mock marriage, I am unable to say, but this much I *do* know—that this moment, with the whole wretched past looming up before me—the years of suffering and ignominy—I love him better than all above or below. But this man, my employer, I detested. His glowing picture of a life of luxury only filled me with disgust. It was no virtue to resist, for a crust alone would have brought to me greater comfort than all the wealth of the Indies shared with him.

Summoning all my courage, I said to the villain, who had never taken his eyes from my face, evidently striving to bring all his magnetic power to bear upon my peculiar temperament —

"'Sir, I am astonished that a man occupying your position in society, representing himself as a Christian gentleman, should so far forget what belongs to decency. I scorn both you and your proposal; and now do me the kindness to leave the house immediately. Not a word,' I continued, as he seemed inclined to argue the point. He attempted to seize my hand. I saw from the frenzied look on his face that the man had determined to do me harm; so, taking advantage of a moment's hesitation on his part, I sprang to the door, opened it, and never stopped until I had reached the street and hidden myself in a neighboring area, and there waited for him to come out. In a moment or two he passed, and I ran back to my little room, locked the door, and waited, in a state of mind impossible to describe, for the arrival of my old friend.

"'Ah, child!' said she, 'I could ha' told you so. Heigho! That's the way with all the big bugs!

A woman's virtue is no more account to 'em than the dirt under their feet; and you have lost your nice work too; mark my words, child. He'll hunt you down; a disappointed man is worse than a baffled beast, because he's got what the beast haint, reason to back him.'

"I had not thought of the work; but now what should I do? No one would make a favorite of me, and give me choice work and ample remuneration, unless he had his own selfish and lustful desires to gratify. What wonder that I could see nothing but desolation before me? I finished the work I had on hand, and returned it, recieved from the book-keeper my money, and was politely informed that my services were no longer needed. I had saved up thirty dollars, and, with this to depend upon, I hunted for employment. Shirts from six to ten cents apiece was the best I could find, and with this I had to be content. My little fund was at last all gone — and work as fast as I could, and as long as I could, I was not able to earn enough to pay our board. The old woman was a good, kind soul, and for three or four weeks did all in her power to encourage me; but she had no income except that obtained by fine washing and ironing for a few families. One day she was taken seriously ill, and my baby also. Neither of us had a cent of money. The next day both invalids were worse. I went to the different stores where we were accustomed to buy our provisions, hoping they would trust me, but met with no success. In despair I begged, but no one would listen to me. Evening came again, and, what with my long fast and dreadfully nervous condition, I had no milk for my baby; and my old friend lay groaning, and almost dying for the comforts of life. I started out again, this time determined to return with food and medicine. I went into a corner grocery, watched my opportunity, hid a loaf of bread under my shawl, and slipped out. I had not got a block from the store, when a policeman clapped his hand upon my shoulder, and, with 'Come with me, miss,' led the way to the station-house, where I was locked up for the night."

CHAPTER VII.

OH! what a night of horror was that! I told the policeman who took me to the dreadful place that I had a starving infant at home, and my only friend was dying for want of care and medicine. I failed to make the least impression upon the stony-hearted man.

"'Come along, now; step up lively; might as well save your gab,' were the only replies he vouchsafed me. Once I tried to run away from him, but he grasped my wrist with his iron hand until I cried out with pain, and then laughed heartily at my suffering. Did you ever"— and her dark eyes sought mine wistfully—"see the inside of a station-house of an evening? I realized by my own wretchedness before this, the fearful amount of suffering there must be in the world, but this experience shut and bolted a

door in my soul that I do not believe will ever
be opened again in this world or the next. It
hardened me. Talk about hell," she continued,
rising and pacing the floor as these terrible
memories again assumed life and shape. "New
York City is full of purgatories, and the station-
houses are not among the least of them. About
ten o'clock a pleasant-faced policeman came in,
and looked around at the strange crowd, it
seemed to me, with an expression which had
some humanity in it, if not pity. I beckoned
for him to come to me, and I told him my
trouble.'

"'Then you really took the loaf of bread?' he
asked.

"'Oh, yes, sir,' I replied. 'I took it because
I had no money to pay for it, and we were all
starving.'

"'Poor child,' he said, musingly. 'Give me
your number, and I'll stop there as I go down
and take them something to eat. It is not likely
that the Dutchman will appear against you in
the morning, and you'll get home in pretty good
season;' and then he went out and returned in

a moment with a piece of gingerbread, which I can tell you I was very thankful for. 'Now,' said he, 'I will be at your house in ten minutes and will make it all right with the old woman and baby.' Oh, I hope," she continued, tears rolling down her cheeks, "that I shall sometime have it in my power to repay that policeman! or at least let him know how heartily I appreciated his kindness. Oh, my friend, such men are few and far between. I thought it would never be morning, and then it seemed to me I should never be called to court, but after a while fifteen or twenty women were placed in marching order, and I one of the number, arrested for taking a loaf of bread, which I could neither beg nor purchase. As the policeman had hinted, no accuser came, and about eleven o'clock I was dismissed. It did seem to me that I should never live to reach home, short as the distance was. My baby lay on the bed by the side of the old woman. A porringer containing some milk, with which the good old soul had fed the little one, with some crumbs of bread, were also beside her. My baby laughed and held up her tiny

hands as I entered, and in my gladness to find
that all was well with the darling, I pressed her
a moment to my heart without bestowing so
much as a glance at the motionless figure of my
friend! Oh, my dear madam, when I *did* look,
I thought I should have fallen **dead** to the floor!
There **lay** the only friend **I had** on earth, her
hand even then clutching the spoon with which
she had kept the breath of life in my baby, her
eyes stony and wide open, and not one trace of
life visible on her features; her hands were cold
and rigid. Death **must have come** to her very
gently two or three hours previous. I called for
assistance, and after a while got together two or
three friends of the old woman's, who arranged
everything in decency and in order. This
paralyzed me. I was like one walking in a
dream. Whatever I did was performed me-
chanically. The funeral **was** over, the body
consigned to the dirt of Potter's Field, the few
little articles of furniture sold to pay expenses,
and I found myself once more, with my infant
in my arms, without **a** friend **and** without a
dollar. Several families offered me washing,

but they objected to the baby. I knew it was useless to attempt that sort of work, as I had never done a day's washing in my life and of course I could never give satisfaction. I walked around for two days, calling at different houses, trying to obtain a chambermaid's situation, but no one wanted an unrecommended female, with a helpless little one. Well, night came again. I was tired and hungry, and had arrived where I cared very little what happened to me. I begged. No one noticed me, and finally I decided to jump into the river. I turned out of Broadway into Cortlandt street, and a block down met a handsomely-dressed woman, who very kindly stopped at my call. She listened to my story, and told me to follow her, and she would put me in the way of earning my own living, and a good one. I knew what she meant, but I didn't care. There was nothing (this I solemnly swear) between that and a double crime — suicide and murder. This was the only thing, my friend, God had left for me to do, and I accepted it gladly. There now, don't shudder so," as a convulsive tremor passed over me.

"Hunger and cold and death are wonderfully strong provocations to this description of sin. I accepted it gladly, because there was nothing else under heaven I *could* do to save my own and my child's life, and hundreds of women are yearly driven to prostitution and the wages of sin for the same reason. Well, I went home with the stranger, found everything in splendid style, a large drawing-room elegantly furnished, and all the apparent paraphernalia of wealth. My baby was given into the hands of a nurse, and the mistress of the establishment superintended my toilet. I can tell you I was dazzlingly arrayed and well fed. I was draped in the costliest of silks and the fleeciest of laces. Diamonds sparkled from my neck and fingers, and as I gazed at myself in the full-length mirror I wondered at my own beauty. I saw the woman pour a drop or two of some white liquid into the fragrant coffee, but I din't know what it was, and didn't care. Oh, how my cheeks burned and eyes glowed after that meal. Had I been sipping nectar from the ambrosial fount, or suddenly transported into some tropical clime, where everything was love and beauty, I could not have experienced more ecstatic sensations. I was taken to the parlors and formally introduced as Miss Belle Hosmer. I played the piano, danced, sung and coquetted, and was, of course, the feature of the evening. It is no use to go on. The next morning found me sorrowful and conscience-stricken, and unable to look into the innocent eyes of my baby. But my virtue was gone. I had sold it for something to eat and a shelter. It was too late to retract, and what if I did? There was nothing else in life for me. From that time to this, weary, heartsick, cursing my existence, I have practiced this dreadful business, but never once, so help me Heaven, because it afforded me pleasure. Now, you have it all, and I suppose realize how useless it will be to think of such a thing as reformation. I am so grateful to you for your kindness and sympathy — but — but"—

"No buts in the case," I replied cheerfully. "Now let me talk."

CHAPTER VIII.

YOU know, as well as you know that you have life and feeling, that the course you have pursued for the last few years is not only destructive to the body, which God gave you to care for and keep pure, but also destructive to your soul. By soul, I mean the higher, more exalted portion of your nature. Anything from which our understanding and heart revolt we should avoid, even if in so doing we die daily and at last literally. I believe, as you say, that hundreds of women are driven to prostitution from the effects of want, grim hunger, and cold, and therefore have not a word to say in regard to your past life; but the present is mine. In a strange but loving manner, Heaven has directed my steps in your direction, and I cannot—*will not*—leave you to follow a business which must send you to your grave dishonored, leaving only a heritage of infamy to your dear little daughter."

"There is no help for it," she sighed. "Grateful as I am for your sympathy and kindness, I can make no promises. God knows, I would be glad to do differently, but what is there in life for a woman after she has once fallen? You know too well that her course is down, down, forever down. Society allows her no alternative."

"But you have set aside all social laws in the past, why not ignore conventionalisms still further, by daring to turn your back upon all such influences, and by respecting yourself? Let society go its own way, where your conscience and common-sense approve. Why should you care what the world says or does? You certainly are not mindful of its requirements now; a pure life need make you no more so; and just remember, as I have told you before, that you have no right to expect anything from social etiquette, excepting so far as you conform to social rules. Notwithstanding your intimacy with sin, it would, I know, grieve you fearfully, did you think that Mary would ever be led to follow in your footsteps."

"Oh, God forbid!" she moaned, clasping her hands convulsively.

"Well, then, you certainly cannot blame other mothers for wishing to keep their daughters away from influences which they know to be unhallowed. It is right for them to be thus particular!"

"Why not put the boot on the other foot a while?" she queried. "Women are only fearful about those of their own sex. It doesn't matter to them how many libertines they entertain;" and now her eyes flashed fire. "The more conquests a man has made, the more ruins he has effected, the better his recommendation to genteel society; but his victims—where are they? A reformed rake, so an old writer puts it, 'makes the best kind of husband,' but who ever heard of a reformed prostitute making a good wife? Pshaw! how ridiculous to talk on so one-sided and unjust a subject. I tell you, madam, there is no chance for a woman in the world."

"I have thought this matter over thousands of times, and deplored the existence of such a state of things in this enlightened and intelligent age, but this is my rock," I replied. "And it is a glorious one to anchor to. It is none of our business what Tom, Dick, or Harry does, how much sin they are guilty of, or how much their commissions are winked at, but it *is* our business what we ourselves are guilty of, because, in a large sense of the word, we are our own keepers, and consequently our responsibility can scarcely be estimated. We must leave off thinking of other people's digressions from rectitude, and the manner in which such digressions are received, and weed the garden of our own souls carefully, not forgetting all the time to sow the seeds of charity. Thus we shall be enabled to do ourselves and others justice."

"A very good doctrine to preach," she answered; "but I am fearful it will hardly work well. You never were tempted; you never were tried; you never were hungry and cold; you never had a little one crying for food you were unable to furnish. What do you know of the awful ills of life? Delicately reared, well cared for, sheltered from every rough wind, how can you judge for me?" and now the lines around the sufferer's mouth grew hard and ominously distinct.

Notwithstanding the unquiet look on my friend's face, I could not refrain from smiling, as I remembered how sorrow and keen soul-trials sometimes develop selfishness, and I went back four years before, to my own heart-ache, my own dark hours, and—as I *then* thought—unparalleled wretchedness, and recalled the tempests of passion, the fearful struggles between desire to leave a world I considered so unfairly governed, and the duty I owed to the life a higher Power had given me to nourish and care for. She saw my smile, and, with her peculiarly keen intuition, remarked eagerly:

"Your expression says, 'I do know something of the storms of life.' Tell me, dear madam, have you ever suffered any sorrow that can be compared to mine?"

I realized that a leaf from my own experience would be of use, and replied:

"Like you I have been hungry and cold. I have not only put one babe to bed unfed, but four precious little ones. Like you I have had no shelter. Our histories differ essentially; but I truly believe that there has been as much wormwood and gall compressed into a few years of my life as into your own, sad as I realize your case to have been."

"And yet you maintained your own self-respect?" she half queried and half affirmed, bursting into tears.

".Yes, my dear, not only my 'own self respect,' but have lived to thank God for those moments of anguish, realizing fully the good they have done me. Nothing can develop a nature like sorrow. Sunshine may do for a while, but the land which does not receive the pelting storm as well as the gentle dew never amounts to much, and its grain is not worth the last threshing."

Just then I heard some one run quickly up stairs; saw my companion's cheek pale, and in a second she had started for the door; but she was too late. The visitor entered hurriedly. I looked up and recognized (how I should like to write his name in letters of fire) a MINISTER, a man who professes belief in the hottest kind of eternal damnation, and whose pleasure it is to shake his congregation over the bottomless pit on all occasions. For a moment he was speechless. Then his old hypocritical manner returned, and with it his self-possession.

"Oh! good afternoon," he blarneyed, walking toward me with outstretched hand, which, by the way, I didn't see, just about then. "I am very glad to meet you here." Then, turning to the agitated woman, who was still standing by the door, he said, blandly: "Mary, I have come to see if you could make me a dozen shirts." Then, looking around to my corner, continued, while his eyes rested everywhere but upon my face: "I have been interested for some time in this young woman, and have striven to do her what little good lay in my power, and "——

"And," said I, taking up the little conjunction, "it is entirely unnecessary for the Rev. Mr. —— to add another lie to his already overflowing list. I perfectly understand the nature of your business here this afternoon; and do me the favor to leave immediately. Mary is my exclusive property now, and desires never to see your face again."

CHAPTER IX.

THE clergyman made a hasty exit, leaving me in a perfect whirlwind of rage. It was distressing enough to think that men who stood high as merchants and citizens should thus seek to ruin both body and soul of the woman I was anxious to befriend, and, if possible, save; but to realize that men wearing God's livery, and professing to be interested for the salvation of all mankind, could thus desire to prey upon the lambs of the fold, was something which my graceless nature could neither understand nor forgive.

Since then I have believed in total depravity, everlasting destruction, and a host of terrible theological Scyllas, which my little religious yacht—notwithstanding the head-wind and tide it had been compelled to buffet—had always steered clear of. But now, where was I? In a malëstrom of doubt and suspicion; for such experiences are enough to make one lose faith in all humanity.

It was some time after the villain left before a word was spoken. Mary was first to break the silence.

"I am not sorry this has happened," she said evidently only half understanding my enraged expression.

"Did you know that man was a so-called minister of the gospel?" I inquired, looking into the eyes which had been full of tears ever since the arrival of her visitor.

"I did," she replied.

"And you knew his real name?"

"I did."

"He did not attempt to deceive you, then?"

"Please do not ask me any more questions!" she answered, beseechingly. "But you might just as well make up your mind that the most of the godliness professed by these pious folks is a sham. My experience taught me that a good while ago, and, as you may imagine, I know considerable about it by this time—more, probably, .

than you ever will. It is only necessary to make
a stunning profession, and then the hypocrite,
entirely covered by his long cloak, looks one
thing and practices another, and gets the credit
of being a meek and lowly Christian. Discouraging, isn't it?"

"Yes, Mary," I replied, "it is discouraging;
facts like these are enough to drive one wild; but
I am thankful I happened to be here. The
wretch wont have much peace of mind for a
while, I reckon."

"Probably he will be somewhat alarmed for
his reputation," said Mary. "But reflection will
soon convince him that his artillery is too heavy
for you to interfere with."

That was undoubtedly so, and the thought
was driven home to my soul.

Of what earthly use is it for one poor, weak
woman to make war against immorality! It
seemed to me on that occasion like throwing
straws against the wind, and in my heart-aching
perplexity I felt very much like abandoning the
ship. To add to my misery, my companion, who
had scarcely taken her eyes from my face since
the villain's exit, remarked, —

"The more, my dear lady, you lift the curtain which has hitherto shut out these unpleasant pictures, the more harassed and perplexed you will become; and I see now, by your weary, distressed expression, that you realize the utter impossibility of making any headway in the work you have undertaken. Let *me* advise you a little now. You are a mother, with children, the most of them boys. To make them what you desire will certainly require all the time you can spare from earning their bread and butter. Then, you are not physically strong, and your health consequently needs the tenderest care, if you would live to see your children grown and educated. Now this work—noble and glorious though it be! —is not for you. You are too sensitive, and your sympathies are too easily enlisted; besides, the views of life which these pictures disclose will have a tendency to make you distrustful, and, for that reason, dreadfully uncomfortable. My dear lady, I am more thankful for the kindness and real love you have shown me than I can ever express, and really have too much regard for yourself and your precious little ones not to

warn you that no good will ever result to yourself from these efforts in this world, and as for
the next, I don't believe much about it. If I
could see the least particle of justice anywhere
I should not be thus sceptical."

"Lord, let me not be discouraged!" was my
especial prayer on that occasion. "Give me
strength to battle for the right! Give me power
to be heard! Make the woman before me powerless to resist the influence I am endeavoring to
sustain, and, above all things, let me be constant,
in season and out of season, in my strivings to be
of benefit to the down-trodden and fallen of my
own sex!"

"I ought, perhaps, to be very thankful to the
man for showing me so plainly the strength of
the fortification I seek to demolish," I remarked,
after she had finished speaking. "I shall
probably be able to look at this matter more
philosophically after a while; and now, Mary, for
yourself. Whatsoever my hands find to do, that,
with God's help, I mean to do. He must have
directed my steps here; and please look me in
the face while I tell you that I have determined

that nothing shall send me from you until I have accomplished my desires, unless it be your own determination."

"Then you will never go," she replied, deeply affected. "But I have spoken for your own good and comfort. You must remember, my friend, that I have tried everything within the scope of my ability — have used every means in my power before I arrived at this dreadful place — to earn a decent living for myself and child; and as true as we both live, just so true, I did not come to prostitution because I liked it, but because, as I have told you several times before, there was nothing else left. If there was nothing then — *then*, before I had fallen — what can there be now?" and a sad smile illumined the intelligent face. "You are a very agreeable lunatic, my dear, but a lunatic, nevertheless!"

"If I will see that you are provided with means to live — with remunerative employment, will you stop, and keep out of this infamous business?" I inquired, noting every change that passed over her countenance.

"How can you ask me such a question?" she

inquired, hastily rising and crossing the room. 'Don't you see that I abhor the life? Merciful God—yes!" she ejaculated, clasping her hands prayerfully. "And can *you* do this?"

"I can, and I will!"

One quick, impetuous, thankful cry, and my companion was close in my embrace. "Woman fashion," methinks I hear some of you say. Yes, woman fashion—and angel fashion this time—for I know that hosts of the bright-winged messengers looked down and smiled, and that the Good Father himself was glad.

CHAPTER X.

THE promise I had desired to gain was mine, and, as I bade my newly-found friends good-by for a day or two, my feelings were of a decidedly mixed character. Thankfulness was, of course, predominant; but, to save my life, I could not help thinking of the man who drew the largest prize in that lottery we have all heard so much about—that mythical elephant, the height of the poor fellow's ambition, but so awkward to handle.

I had started out one day to gain some information from beggars, determined to question all who approached me, and, as a friendly paper remarked, "went home with the first one met." The journal refrained from saying, "woman fashion." It was a male (*Mail*) editor, too, who stopped thus considerately short in his criticism, and I shall always admire him for his self-denial.

Well, when I arrived home, I surveyed my little family (" little " in this case is a word not at all meant for a descriptive adjective) and wondered what I should do first. I had realized from the beginning how difficult it would be to provide remunerative work for one so totally unskilled in every department of labor. I knew that it would be a long time (perhaps never) before she could support herself; and, with her independent ideas, I saw plainly that not a little finesse would have to be practiced, if I would have the object of my solicitude comfortable. To interest my friends in the case would involve too much publicity at this critical juncture.

" Do not, *please* do not, bring any one to see me!" was her especial prayer, and who could but respect the extremely natural wish! I hadn't a friend but would believe every incident I might relate to them — but would help me in caring for these new responsibilities; still, it would certainly be very unfair not to allow them a glimpse of the person they would benefit. So, after mature deliberation, I concluded (*this* time not " woman fashion ") to keep the story to myself, and try three or four brokers who had previously come to my rescue in cases of destitution.

The woman's whole condition must be changed. Her surroundings must undergo an immediate and thorough transformation; and, as I put down the figures in my little account-book, reckoning up the expense of coal, wood, a new carpet, a stove, flour, hominy, and decent clothes, to save my life I couldn't make it less than one hundred and fifty dollars. If I omitted my daily walk and hour or so of conversation; if I retired later and rose earlier,— it would take a long time to make that amount over and above my own large and necessary expenses. To cap the climax, my four-year old, who had been teasing for a doll that opened its eyes, and had long, curly, *real* hair, came to my side just as I had added the last domestic necessity, with,—

"Mamma, when may I have my doll-baby? Didn't you say when you got that last 'tory done?"——

"Yes, dear," I answered, and wondering, as I kissed her rosy lips, if, under the circumstances, the darling should not be indefinitely put off. Oh these everlasting questions of duty and inclination! Then master Joe, a young autocrat of six, approached.

"Mamma, see the hole that's just this moment come on my knee. Mamma, I want *boots* next time. Don't you remember you *said* you'd buy me boots when these were worned out? but look at 'em!" And Josie's shoe, with the toe entirely stubbed out, was held up to view.

I declare if, the remainder of that day, every member of my own family, and every person of my acquaintance didn't either want something that I was expected to furnish, or else had unredeemed promises to remind me of! I believe it is always thus.

Some one will probably suggest that no person is excusable for attempting to take more of a burden upon himself than he is able to carry. Perhaps not; but contact with the rough edges of the world has taught me this much, — that if our poor, sick, and imbecile waited for the strong and wealthy to take their cases in hand, they'd *wait*. This woman and child I had accepted as a direct present from the hand of God, and

if nothing else would do, I would divide with
her; but if not, it could be avoided, because, as
I looked at the flaxen heads ranged around, with
their toys and books, and noted their precious
youthful prattle, I understood my first duty.
And so I thought late into the night, and the
decision my heart and conscience arrived at was
to go begging next day, and raise money enough
to make the desired improvement in my friend's
condition.

I wonder if every one hates to beg as I do?
Once, in the extremest want, I was offered a soliciting position in a certain suburban church, for
which said church would fairly remunerate me.
I started, "solicited" just three times, and returned to the worthy deacon with my letters of introduction, saying, 'mid a storm of tears in which
I am forced to admit there was quite as much
temper as sorrow, "Sir, I am much obliged to
you; but I'd rather starve, freeze, be burnt at the
stake, and suffer a pretty warm purgatory, and"—

"Yes, my dear madam," he interrupted, well
understanding my vulnerable spot. "But your
children?"

"I don't care! I'll put every one of them in an orphan asylum, and take in house-cleaning, before I'll do any more of it." And I walked from the deacon's presence, without a dollar in my pocket. The good man evidently thought me a proper candidate for Bloomingdale.

I wonder how folks continually do so many things from which their natures revolt! I wonder if it will always be so! I wonder if we take **poverty and** misery over the river with us!

CHAPTER XI.

THERE was no time to be lost. My two newly-assumed responsibilities must be cared for, and that immediately; so the next morning I started for Wall street on my "soliciting" expedition. The men whom I most relied upon for aid were not at their respective offices. "On the street," I was informed: "Over to the Stock Exchange," "Be in presently;" and so I walked on to the corner of Broad and Wall, and looked down on to the sea of black hats in front of that elegant building around which Bulls and Bears do congregate, and wished that it were possible for soul to speak to soul in some wordless electrical manner, and that the owners of those beavers and felts might be directed to file past the apple-stand, by which I stood ruminating, and, sympathizing with my great desire to aid the unfortunate, place in my hands plentiful means for so doing;

and for a moment, forgetful of haste and necessity, I stood gazing at the telegraph wires and
considering how news was transmitted from individual to individual, from state to state, and
from the new to the old world, and marvelling
at the genius and learning which had brought
the widely separated into such intimate and
glorious connection; and then I wondered why
a man or woman with quick, loving sympathies,
and moral earnestness, might not be a sufficiently powerful battery to so act upon the in-
visible wires, which connect brain with brain and
heart with heart, as to make speech and solicitation
unnecessary. But the crowd kept up its auction-
eer-like howling, and I was nothing but a little
speck in the universe,— a very important speck
in my own estimation,— with no power to attract,
orreach the great heart of humanity, except
with my tongue, and that tiny member, generally willing to play its part in the great drama
of life, never felt less like wagging than on this
long-to-be-remembered occasion. I was growing metaphysical. That would never do. The
buxom old apple-woman, quite as deep in the

bustle of trade as her more reckless brother down the street, looked at me wonderingly. I walked on a few steps, and presently a cheery voice said:

"Good morning, Mrs. Kirk; I am blessed if I wasn't thinking of you just a moment ago!" and a kind hand grasped mine. One of the individuals I was looking for, you see. "All well at home, I hope," he continued. "Little folks smart? You look sad — no trouble, I trust?"

"We are all in usual health," I replied, "but I came over this morning on purpose to see you. Can you spare me five minutes at the office?"

"Yes, my dear child, thirty of them, if you will excuse me while I deposit this troublesome stock. Dame Erie has been on a regular bender this last week; old enough to know better, you understand, but she keeps me stepping round pretty lively; walk right down to the office, and I'll be with you in a jiffy."

"I hope Erie has treated *you* very well," I remarked as, a few moments after, he seated himself by my side.

"What poor unfortunate is in a tight place

now?" he inquired, good-naturedly. "I know *somebody* is in need, by the looks of your face. Yes, Erie, the jilt, thanks to a bright eye to the windward, has treated me uncommonly well; and now, tell me who's in trouble, and all about it. It is rather curious that I should have been thinking about you this morning."

I had only now to relate that part of my story I had thought best to impart. The responsive chord was struck without a word, and I was soon in the midst of my narrative.

"Bless your heart, yes! made *comfortable?*— of course she shall be! By George! that is wonderful! I suppose there are hosts of just such cases in this modern Sodom," he interrupted, as I stopped to take breath. "Glad you came to me. Let's see: how much money ought to do this? Have you made any calculation? Two hundred dollars, eh? That ought to fix things up a little, I should think. Good gracious, the poor child is actually weeping!" as I turned my head to hide the tears of thankfulness.

Two hundred dollars! To have raised *half* that sum I expected to have been compelled to

make at least four "soliciting" visits, and what
wonder I was glad when begging was so distaste-
ful! My friend did not begin to comprehend the
depth of my gratitude. How could he? Conventionalisms, as wicked as they are stupid, came
in to prevent any real heartfelt demonstrations;
but he will know all about it some day, not
perhaps until we have both stepped over to the
great other side; but I'll show him then, see
if I don't. As I passed out he recalled me
with,—

"Look here; I bought my sister, a year ago, a
real nice Wheeler and Wilson sewing-machine.
Her health is very delicate, and she is not able to
use it at all. If it would be of any service to her,
she can have it and welcome; and also all the
work of our family, that is, if she proves herself
a good and reliable seamstress, which I have no
doubt she will."

God hadn't opened that door wide. It **was**
not even ajar; no indeed! The portals were
thrown open and relief had come rolling in,
in a manner totally unexpected. It is perhaps
unnecessary to state that I accepted the ma-

6

chine, and with it more faith in God, and more in humanity. I went my way rejoicing. Yes, I mean it,—more faith in God; although I am aware that expression is not exactly orthodox. A Christian's faith should be just as bright through the clouds and pelting rain, through the thunder-storms of trouble, through death and disaster, as when the sunshine of happiness irradiates and makes glad the soul; at least, I suppose it should be, but I cannot make it seem exactly natural. Wouldn't it be nice to take a peep behind the great black curtain, and see what it all means?

I found my friend anxiously awaiting my arrival, her dark eyes full of that new light of hope and determination which had dawned for the first time the day before. I went about my little comforts and improvements with as light a heart as if this tumble-down old shanty had been an establishment on Fifth avenue, and I its proprietor. It was the home of virtue and peace, and I hoped to make it one of contentment.

CHAPTER XII.

I HAVE been asked several times by those who have become interested in this story, how I dared trust the woman I was striving to assist, and if I felt no misgivings as to her ability to keep the promise she had made me. To all I would say that no doubt of her desire to lead a different life ever entered my head from the first moment I laid my eyes on her face, and it would have made no difference in my endeavors had I been suspicious of failure. You who are sceptical in regard to the reformation of such, select a case and do your best with it, and if you do not discover a host of things to love and respect in the object of your solicitude, your experience will be vastly different from mine.

I had left my friend comfortable, and my next move was to purchase some plain, tasteful dresses for both mother and child, and prepare the latter for a good public school, which she was extremely anxious to attend. What with my own work and the delay of shopping, it was some three or four days before I found it convenient to call again. Early one morning I was surprised by a visit from my little protege.

"Why, Mary," said I, as the child ran into my room, "I am glad to see you; but what is the matter?"

The darling's eyes were red and swollen from weeping, and her whole manner gave evidence of great mental excitement.

"Oh," she answered, "mother is very sick; I don't know what ails her! She was all right till yesterday. See what she made for me out of one of the dresses you brought; don't it look nice?" and the little one displayed the neatly-fitting calico with a pride which did my heart good to witness. "It is a long time since mother sewed a stitch for me. I hope these wont be the last now," and the poor over-wrought child broke completely down.

"Tell me all about it, dear, and then I will get ready and go home with you." After a little I listened to the following, which I will give in her own words as nearly as I can remember:

" I thought mother was going to be happy now, we had got things so nice; but she has looked sadder than ever, and I couldn't get her to talk much; but she kept to work until last night, and then, all of a sudden, fell over in her chair. Oh dear! I thought she was dying! I tried to lift her up, but she was too heavy. I bathed her face with cold water, and after a little she roused up and said: ' Oh, Mary! Mary! you poor little outcast! if I die, promise me that you will find your father.' Oh, my dear Mrs. Kirk!" and now the child's arms were around my neck. " I hope that God will forgive me, for I was very wicked to my poor sick mother, but, when she said that—'*find my father*'—I thought I should have died for very madness. You see I always knew that I must have had a father, and I also knew that he wasn't dead; and from little things here and there, I got it into my head that he left my mother because he got tired of her, or something else; and then to have her ask me to find him if she died was a little too much for this child, and I told her that I'd be torn into inch pieces first. Find a man who would leave his wife and child to starve!" and the dark eyes flashed forth a light which transformed the little one into an earnest, impassioned, determined woman.

"But, child," said I, "you surely didn't say those bitter things to your mother, and she so sick, did you?"

"Yes, I did," she replied, dashing away the tears, — "yes, I did, and that's what I am sorry for; because I expect she didn't half know what she was talking about, and ever since she has kept straight at it. Her hands are hot as fire, and so is her head. I got old Mother Thurston to sit with her while I came over for you."

"Mary," said I, taking the child's trembling fingers in mine, "have you the least idea who your father is?"

"No, ma'am," she replied; "and more than that, I don't want to have. It seems to me, ma'am, and I can't get it out of my head, that he is the cause of all the dreadful trouble we have had, and I hate him! Wont you please to tell me what you think about it?"

"I know more, perhaps, about the circumstances

than you do, my dear," I replied, striving to
suppress all emotion, and impressed with the
necessity of imparting some idea of the past to
the little one. Ever since I had listened to the
woman's sad story, a feeling of pity had stolen
into my heart for the man who had wrought this
great misery. I could not rid myself of it, nor,
to save my life, bring myself to feel that he was
as recklessly guilty as the facts seemed to warrant.
That he loved the mother of this little one, I
knew. From her own description I realized that
the affection was not merely an animal or sensual
one. It appeared to me that, suffering from the
effect of an unhappy marriage, with an aching
heart and a hungry soul, he had met this beautiful girl, fallen desperately in love, and believed
that, with his wondrous wealth and the great
love she felt for him, he could keep the matter
of his first matrimonial experience secret. I realized, too, that it was a dastardly act for any one
to be guilty of, but I pitied him nevertheless.
So I said to the little one, scarcely conscious of
the import of my words: "My dear, never let
me hear you say again that you hate your father.
I do not know who he is, or where he is, but I

know he does not hate you, and I believe that had he known where to have found you all these years, you would not have been left to suffer so; and more than all, child, I am strongly led to believe that you will be very proud of him one of these days."

The child hung her head for a moment, and then replied, while her eyes twinkled with pleasure: "What a funny lady you are. I have got something in my pocket I want to show you. I wasn't going to, because I thought maybe it would be doing mother a wrong. I can't read or write much, but mother cries over this every night; I've caught her at it lots of times."

I took the note, soiled with frequent usage, and read, while my heart almost stopped beating. It was simply an affectionate excuse for not returning at the promised time. It was signed "Your own Charles," and under this was written in the woman's own chirography "Alla ——" a name with which I was almost as familiar as with my own. A name representing money, philanthropy, position, and all sorts of good things. A man of whom I had never heard the first whisper of evil.

CHAPTER XIII.

"WHAT'S the matter, please?" inquired Mary, noticing my surprise. "Is that anybody you know? Do tell me quick!" she continued, imploringly. "You don't half feel how mother's strange actions hurt me. There are two or three things she has cried over ever since I can remember, and now they are driving her mad. You understand what all this means; do tell me. I am not a little girl like other little girls you are acquainted with. I never was a child; that is, I never cared to play and romp like other children. I never had but one thought, and that was, 'What is the matter with mother?' and if you don't tell me, I shall *die;* indeed I shall!"

The little one's voice trembled with emotion, and tears filled her brilliant eyes. I dared not impart to her my suspicions, or rather my knowl-

(89)

edge; and, after a little evasion, I managed to quiet the child. "I know nothing, Mary, for a certainty," I answered. "Your mother has not given me her confidence, and I am simply doing a good deal of guessing, that is all. You must have patience and wait. It seems to me the clouds are breaking, and, as I have told you before, child though you are, the severest of your trials have been passed."

"But if mother should die, what could there be in life for me?" she sobbed. "I have often prayed that we both might walk out of this cruel world together; but now that things seem to look as if we could live a little bit like decent folks, I did hope there would be no more trouble. I should think whose ever business it is to punish me would be about tired by this time, for I've had nothing but kicks and cuffs ever since I was born till you came and fixed us all up, and mother stopped going out nights and doing the things that made my heart ache, and I began to be what I never was before, happy; and no sooner had I commenced to enjoy myself than something else dreadful turns up. Mother is crazy."

It was no use to quote passages of Scripture to this precocious child, no use to attempt to administer comfort in any ordinary method. She could not be made to understand discipline, as taught by professed Christians of the present day. She was guiltless of intentional wrong: why should she be punished? So, with the little one's hand tightly clasped in mine, I sought once more the abode of my friend. To say that I was startled at the change a few days had accomplished does not half express the state of my feelings. As we entered, she turned her face toward the door and smiled. A single spot of scarlet burned on each cheek, making the remainder of the face still more pallid by contrast. Her long, abundant hair had been released from its coil to relieve the heated brain, and now it rippled over the pillow, giving a weird, almost angelic, appearance to the woman, who seemed, as I examined her condition carefully, to be hovering on the confines of the Eternal City.

"I am so glad you have come!" she said, "so glad! I dreamed that you had left me forever."

"What a stupid dream, to be sure!" I answered,

assuming an indifference I was far from feeling. "You are feverish, Mary. I think you must have taken cold. How long have you felt so miserable?"

"Oh, all along," she murmured; "but then some way I have never allowed my feelings to get the mastery of me until now. I strove against it for your sake, indeed I did; but it would come. I thought to get to work, and hoped to do well, so that you could see how thankful I was for all your kindness, but it was no use; I shall never again be fit for anything but the grave; and for all our sakes, I wish death would come quickly."

"My dear child," said I, gravely, "you are certainly the most ungrateful member of my family. You should not have dared to get ill. Have you any new trouble?" and I took the thin, burning hand in mine, and tried to soothe the over-wrought nerves.

"It is my brain," she replied, drawing my hand to her forehead. "The part of me that thinks, dear. Some way, since I knew that we were provided for, and that Mary hadn't to suffer for something to eat, I have had more time to think, and it almost kills me. The past is dreadful. How much better it would have been for me and her," pointing to the child, who sat on the bed, her eyes full of tears, "if I had, when so sorely oppressed, folded her a little closer to my heart and jumped overboard! God would have forgiven it, I am sure; but now there is nothing for me here or hereafter. A few weeks of madness, and then the miserable flicker will be quenched forever."

"Desperate means for desperate cases," I repeated mentally, realizing that something must be done, and that speedily, or I should never be able to rouse her from the condition which, after all, was an extremely natural one, the only wonder being that she had not succumbed before.

"Of whom have you been thinking?" I inquired, softly, still retaining the hot hand, "for the last few hours?" Again that wan smile, and she whispered, "Oh! of him, you know?"

"Yes, I know," was my reply.

"How can I help it? Sometimes I think," she continued, "that I acted too hastily in leaving him the day that dreadful woman came there. His last words were that he loved me, and I know I loved him, and oh! my Father! I love him now. I wonder if, by and by, after God is satisfied of my sincere repentance for all I have done amiss, he will let me join hands with him and be his friend? Why, I would be willing to wait a thousand years."

More than one severe struggle for calmness I have had during my most eventful life, but this was the most difficult of all. An indescribable something urged me on, and yet, as I looked into her sunken eyes, the idea which had such thorough control of my faculties seemed utterly impracticable. Still, I could not be quiet.

"Why don't you talk to me like you used?" she queried, peeping into my face. "You are discouraged, and I don't wonder."

"Not a bit of it!" said I. "Why, bless your heart, this reaction is no more than a philosopher would have expected." But I was busy with my thoughts. "Mary, you think you have guarded your secret admirably, don't you? I respect the feeling which has made you so careful; but, my

dear, Mr.—— —— is not unknown to me."
Oh, if you could have seen her! I had hit the
right nail that time.

"How came you? What have I ever done?
Where did you find it out? That name never
escaped my lips. Oh! my God! what shall I
do?" and she threw herself away and groaned
aloud. "You would not tell!" she shrieked,—
"you would not dare to tell!"

"Never, my dear child, shall the name escape
my lips, if you do not desire it. But let me
tell you one thing. He is a man of whom I
never heard one evil word spoken. A man who
has the respect of the entire community. Now,
Mary, something must be done. If he ever
cared for you, and I am inclined to think he did,
he cannot have quite forgotten you."

"Hush now! hush! stop it! not a *word!*"
she almost screamed. "Don't you ever dare!
He took me as his mistress when he already had
a wife. Was there any honor about that? No,
indeed! A man of whom you never heard an
evil word! Does society ever say anything of
men who commit such terrible sins as these?   •

Oh no! they are always 'honorable'! and yet I loved him, love him still; but don't you dare, don't you *dare*, I say, ever utter a word of this!"

My first point had been gained. There was something new to be thought about, and I had no fear of insanity just then. So, after a few words of sympathy, I bade her "good-by." Promising to come again soon, I left her to call on the man who had wrought this accumulation of woes.

CHAPTER XIV.

IT seemed to me, as I left the bedside of
the sufferer and walked down the rickety
old stairway into the street, that my feet
scarcely touched the ground. I felt like one up-
borne, upheld — a sort of spiritual exhilaration I
had never before experienced. I was conscious
of a mighty presence, a wonderful power that
made me strong and calm, strangely controlling
my actions. I do not pretend to account for this.
Most of my readers have probably been similarly acted upon in some portion of their lives.
What would I not give, what would I not sacrifice, to push aside the curtain, and observe how
that was accomplished! "Nervously suscepti-
ble," says one; "large clairvoyant powers,"
says another; "a spiritual medium," exclaims
still another. As I look back upon the singular

developments of that day alone, I am lost in wonder and amazement; and confess myself just as ignorant of the *modus operandi* of the concealed wire-pulling of that occasion, as the veriest child who reads these pages. So, call it what you please, account for it, each one, by his or her pet theory: it is all of that and more beside to me; for it makes me certain of a glorious by and by; of loving arms all ready to hold me close; of a Father, lover, and friends; of a heaven where Mary can revel in the purity of her first love, and where you and I may see the crooked things of this life made straight. Just consider a place where mistakes are rectified, angularities rounded off, causes explained, and love our eternal food. Oh, for one draught from that fountain!

As I walked "Up Broadway," determined to get at the depths of the affair that had so long and painfully occupied me, I seemed to meet an entirely different set of people from those who generally promenade this metropolitan thoroughfare. A kind light shone from every eye, a sort of "God bless you" trembled upon every lip; and as I stopped a moment to take breath, and try to explain these singular sensations, a cheery voice sang out,—

"And is it yerself, my dear lady, that can be telling a poor feller, who has lost his way, the straight road to Houston street, sure?"

"Houston street? oh, yes, sir!" I replied, endeavoring to bring myself down to the practical place, from whence issued this pleasant voice. "Houston street is two blocks above," and I pointed in the right direction.

"Thank you, ma'am; thank you, ma'am," he replied, touching his hat respectfully. "I'm much obliged to ye, sure; but is it out o' the clouds ye dropped? for upon the honor of an Irishman, ye have no look like the other folks round here. It wouldn't take a wizard to tell that it is not of *yerself* ye are thinking to-day. God bless you, ma'am, whatever ye are about."

This was a God-speed I had not reckoned upon, and it served a double purpose: first, in bringing me down to the concert pitch and a more thorough realization of the peculiar errand I had started upon, and next, it assured me of success.

That hearty, "God bless you, ma'am," rings in my ears still, and yet my Celtic friend was utterly unconscious of having said or done a pleasant thing. I cannot but think that he was a part of that day's programme, and no insignificant part either. By the time I arrived at my destination, I was conscious that my errand might be construed, by the man I had determined to have an audience with, into a piece of impertinence; but that did not deter me. I was a little less dreamy and poetical, but not a whit less resolved upon accomplishing my purpose. I reached the establishment, entered, and looked carefully around to see if the object of my search was present. Nowhere, to be sure. I don't think my voice trembled a particle as I handed my card to an usher; but the letters which made up "Eleanor Kirk," so plainly embossed upon the enamelled pasteboard, seemed dancing a jig. "Be kind enough to give this to Mr. ——, and tell him that the lady awaits a private interview."

The man gave me a scrutinizing look, as much as to say, "Some woman with an agency, or worse still, on a begging expedition. *You* wont see Mr. —— to-day," and walked rapidly away. He returned in a moment and said,—

"Mr. —— wishes to know the nature of your business; unless it is exceedingly important, he cannot see you, as he is especially engaged at this hour."

I took another card, wrote on the back: "A matter of life and death; a leaf from the past," inclosed it in an envelope, and waited. I was not at all surprised when the usher returned and politely bade me follow him. Something kept saying to my heart, which throbbed in my bosom like a young earthquake (I suppose it was my own spiritualized self) "Keep down; God is with you; hosts of angels are helping you in this. Be steadfast!" and in a moment I stood in the presence of the man who had wrought the terrible desolation I had just left. My first thought, as I scanned this really noble countenance (for I had never had an opportunity of observing him so closely before) was, "Mary, I do not wonder that your young heart went out towards this man; do not wonder that you forsook father and mother, and for his dear sake lived among strangers; do not wonder at your wild idolatry," and then, with these thoughts chasing each other in quick succession through my brain, I stood looking him straight in the eye, without a single word.

"Mrs. or Miss Kirk?" he observed, politely extending his hand, and drawing a chair for me to be seated. Still, I stood like one suddenly struck dumb. Oh! if I could only write out the sermon that came to me on that occasion, I should be doing a good for humanity; but the ideas will not shape themselves into language, and I suppose I shall be compelled to carry it round in my soul until—well, who knows when?

But it is there, and must *sometime* have an airing. I placed my hand in his, and in a twinkling, realized that he comprehended my errand. The soul-telegraph had done its mighty work; and, without more ado (laugh if you please, call it "woman fashion," if you have a mind), I burst into an uncontrollable fit of sobbing, in which — doubt all who may, but the fact is as true as that I am now trying to describe that scene — my companion joined, and this without a word having been spoken. Heaven and earth are full of mysteries, but this episode **of my life** is the most mysterious of all.

CHAPTER XV.

I HAVE always noticed when men and women are similarly affected by sudden grief, in case of death, or other bereavements, that women are the first to recover composure. Now, as far as I have observed — and I have tried to discriminate clearly and conscientiously — the good and bad are about equally distributed, and the counterpart of every wicked man may be found in the opposite sex.

This, I know, will be questioned by many radical reformers, who are somehow determined to see no virtue or decency among the fathers of the nation. The memory of my father — God bless him! — is just as dear to me as that of my mother, and in sympathy and tenderness I believe he was really her equal. Through the numberless ills of childhood, his loving arms encompassed me. Life was dreary, indeed, after he was called away.

It has so happened that in my strange and wearisome pilgrimage, my soul has been cheered by kind-hearted, pure-minded, honor-loving members of the proscribed sex; and I never hear them denounced, as I have lately had occasion to, by women who, if their own statements are to be credited, must have possessed demons for fathers, brothers, and husbands, without feeling that the denouncers are not only shockingly ignorant in regard to natural laws, but also deficient in good, sterling common sense. Why a father should be of less consequence to a child than that child's mother, or his good name less to be considered, is something I cannot yet understand. But what I started to say was this: that the reason women generally recover themselves more quickly is, that care-taking belongs especially to them. The bearing and rearing of children tends to develop this quality, and therefore, the consideration of others, if not the first thought, generally follows closely in its wake. Now I had not the remotest intention of reading a homily upon the virtues of the race, or of attempting to explain the difference between the natures and dispositions of the sexes;

but it seems to me that women should be exceedingly careful how they attempt to underrate the masculine element; and it appears to me also, that women are quite as much to blame for the laxity of morals among men as men themselves. Did women but turn their backs upon known roués and libertines—did they but set the same value upon virtue and nobility of character that they do upon wealth and social position, the attainment of their God-given rights would then be comparatively easy.

There is nothing on earth that so unnerves me as to see a strong man in tears. I had dried my own eyes, and with my hand still in that of the stranger, waiting for him to recover composure, these thoughts chased themselves swiftly through my brain. It is astonishing how much one may think in an instant of time. Social requirements, conventionalities, privileges, each and all took on distinct and aggravated forms; and without the least supernatural prescience, I was enabled perfectly to understand the route which the individual before me had travelled to reach this port of misery and humiliation.

"Pity him?" Yes, with my whole soul; just as much, and just as unreservedly as though the sufferer had been one of my own sex. As I stood (I must confess it) a little out of patience with myself for allowing my heart to go out thus spontaneously to a man who had been the cause of the downfall and degradation of one of my sisters, this little sentence was wafted into my soul— "All one in Christ Jesus;" and that settled it.

After that my hand was passive until he was ready to relinquish it.

"Come now," said I, "let's be seated, and talk this matter over immediately," and I straightened myself up, wiped my eyes for the fortieth time, and endeavored to assume a practical manner, which I imagined must be adopted with the grief-stricken man, but which I was very far from feeling. Not that I felt in the least like shirking the responsibility thus voluntarily assumed—that wasn't it; but I *did* feel strangely like managing the case my own way, and it seemed to me that wouldn't do. I have learned better since; have found that an impulse is oftentimes a genuine inspiration; and that the man or woman who

pushes impulse one side, because Whately or
some other man condemns impulse as contrary to
true logical deduction—that person crowds out
the divinest part of his nature.

"I cannot be mistaken," he said, with a desperate effort to be calm, "in regard to your errand.
Oh! if you only knew what a load of wretchedness I have carried round with me all these years
—if you only knew"—and here the poor fellow
broke down again.

"Good God!" he moaned, now rising and
pacing the room distractedly. "What a life! and
what a wretch! Tell me, and tell me quickly—
tell me this instant"—now seizing both my
hands and drawing me to the centre of the room.
"Where is she? Is she alive? Don't, I implore
you—don't tell me I may never look upon her
face again! If you have come with her dying
message—her precious last words—leave me
without uttering them. As Heaven is my judge,
I could not bear it! Talk about the tortures of
the damned," he continued, more to himself than
to me. "Have I not endured them? and all because of **love**—God-given love, as pure as angels

may feel! It was love, so help me Heaven, it was love that brought all this desolation upon us; and now she is dead — dead — and you have come to tell me so! For pity's sake, why don't you speak?"

"I shall have *two* lunatics on my hands pretty soon, if you do not control yourself, my dear sir," I replied, a strange calm suddenly flooding my soul.

"*Two* lunatics?" he repeated, catching at the words with wonderful rapidity, and drawing a chair close to mine.

"You are smiling, **Mrs. Kirk!** Why, your face looks like the face of heaven after a thunder shower! You couldn't smile if *she* was dead. You couldn't smile if you knew that such news would cause me to blow my brains out! *Two* lunatics? Mary is not in a mad-house! *That* can't be! But that would be better than have her dead, because I could bring her to her reason! Ay, my love could do that! She is alive. Yes, I know she is, by your face! Tell me where I may find her," **and the eager** eyes were fixed upon mine with a magnetism which was irresistible.

"Mary is alive," I replied, and then waited a moment.

"Bless God!" he ejaculated. "Oh! how untiringly I have searched for her, always to be disappointed."

"Mary is alive," I continued, "and in the possession of her senses, but very ill."

"Tell me, Mrs. Kirk, that she is not dangerously ill; and for God's sake let me go to her at once." And the man rushed frantically for his hat.

"But you are in no condition to go into the street," I continued. "Mary is ill, but I think, if you will listen to me for a few moments, I can arrange matters so that you may be able to do her a great deal of good; I do not consider her *dangerously* ill, and I know that joy seldom kills; so please be quiet for a little."

"God bless you for ever and ever," he cried. "I am a happy man already.'

CHAPTER XVI.

HAT a charm there is in silence! What a charm in sympathetic communion! What untold, indescribable happiness in feeling that one has accomplished a little good, and that good appreciated. For weeks I had been quietly and persistently at work, endeavring to benefit the real, true wife of the man I was then sitting by the side of, whose fine eyes seemed to look into my soul and seek the depths of the motives which had actuated me in this case.

Please don't, at this stage of the proceedings, confound terms; because that would scarcely be fair. I say "true wife" for two reasons: the first because of that delightful and glorious blending of soul, that perfect adaptability of mental and physical which goes to make a genuine and God-instituted marriage; and the

second, because, at the time, she honestly considered herself such. My organ of veneration
is not perhaps as large as it would be had I
moulded the bump to suit my own ideas of a
healthy and well-formed phrenological development; but there is one thing which my head
and heart instinctively bow to, and that is the
power of love. That the man beside me had
been guilty of a terrible wrong, there was no
way of dodging, and yet I found myself very
busy making excuses for him. He had sinned,
and sinned for love's sake, and love and I were
on the best of terms; and so I contrasted him
with wretches I had seen and heard of, who
without an atom of affection for those they
had selected for their lustful designs, wooed,
won, and cast aside. I suddenly grew metaphysical, and considered the philosophy of love—
love in its elemental and diviner sense—and
had almost arrived at the sphere where no
other kind is admissible, where the bondage
of clay is forgotten, or if necessarily remembered,
with a joy next akin to ecstacy, that the disci-

pline has past—when my companion remarked
in a low tone,—

"My dear madam, have you quite made up
your mind in regard to my case? Your eyes
have pierced my very soul. It really seeems to
me that there is not a thought there but you
have seen and commented upon. I was thinking," he continued, still in the low, mellifluous
tones, which appeared an index to the man's
sweetness and nobility of disposition, "that
you must, of a necessity, consider me just the
scamp I have proved myself to be, **and** yet
your expression is merciful in the extreme.
Tell me, can you understand a love so deep
so high, so boundless, as to preclude all possibility of any other feeling—a sensation so
all-absorbing, that prudence, propriety, and all
human laws are, if not set at defiance, quite
ignored? Oh! if I could only make you understand that this was the feeling I had for
Mary! Why, my dear woman, so all-absorbing
was it that I had no room for anything else
except, well, except"—and here the low tones
grew almost indistinct, **and** then ceased alto-

8

gether. Just at that very moment I was wondering why he **had** **not** spoken of his child.
Could it be he had forgotten her existence? or
was he purposely waiting for me? There was
the soul-telegraph again; and although the poor
fellow's manner was anxious and flurried, the
nerves of his face twitching with the intensity
of the effort to appear calm, I could not refrain
from smiling as the wonderful power of soul
communication was again brought home to me.
There we sat, looking into each other's faces,
saying, oh, so little, for our hearts **were too**
full for utterance, and yet our souls were just
as sociable as though they had been on intimate
terms ever since their creation. To be a
brilliant conversationalist is certainly the *ne*
plus ultra of accomplishments, but to be able
to talk sensibly and brilliantly without words
of a verity, transcends that; but then there are
so few whose magnetism will allow of this
perfect and glorious understanding. "Why
do you smile, Mrs. Kirk?" was the next question, asked with quivering lip.

"Because, dear sir, the metaphysical part of

this strange experience pleases me to such a wonderful extent that I cannot help it. We seem to be, as the Spiritualists say, perfectly *en rapport;* and now you would have me tell you of your little girl—your dear little girl, the dearest little girl of my acquaintance, the one who first took me to your—your wife."

Oh! how I wish you who read this, you whose sympathies are with both these sufferers, could have looked into the face of my companion, as I uttered those words! For a moment he did not speak, then leaning forward inquired almost in a whisper, "How big is she?"

Comprehending the depth of feeling which sought expression in this extremely commonplace inquiry, I replied, "About *so* big," raising my arm to the little one's height.

"Is she healthy, and strong, and bright?," was the next question, in the same eager tones. A vision of the little one as I had first seen her, curled up on the steps of the Central National, shivering with cold, and almost starved, was brought distinctly before my mind's eye. Just to think of it — the daughter of one of our most favored metropolitan merchants, in want of the commonest necessaries of life! The child of love too, and perfect confidence! What could it all mean? Why the necessity of such torture to one of God's little ones? The child, with her bright, beautiful eyes, glaring at me from their framework of long, tangled hair, her naive, almost brusque manner, wonderful logic of her reasoning, the wit, which contact with the rough edges of the world had made as keen as a two-edged sword, all came back to me, and I replied, with a perfect knowledge of my subject, "Yes sir, she is healthy, and strong, and bright." I could not bring my, self to tell him the thoughts which were thus uppermost in my mind. "Let the past pass in review slowly," was my mental determination, endeavoring to evade the eyes which, somehow, would persist in their steadfast inspection.

"Will you tell me how my little daughter looks?" was the next query. "Like her mother or father?"

"Very much like both," I made answer.

" She has her mother's features with your expression; and really it is extremely hard to tell which she most resembles."

" And will you be kind enough to inform me where you first met her; how it happened that you became interested in my darlings? I see that you are fearful of wounding my feelings by too frank an explanation of circumstances."

There it was again; more telegraphing. The science of clairvoyance had always been a pleasant study to me, although I had never learned to discriminate where clairvoyance began and a vivid imagination ended. To place implicit reliance upon the phenomena I had seen and heard described savored of over-credulity, and that I might not be too easily swayed by the mysterious and apparently unexplainable, I had always compelled myself to stop and reason sternly upon every subject presented. It was not wonderful that my companion should imagine, or rather suspect a great many dreadful things in reference to the woman and child so long separated from him; but it *was* wonderful that his mind should thus closely follow mine. So far there had been no mistake.

" My little one was cold and hungry when you found her. Aye ! you need not answer, your eyes brimming with tears is enough for me. My God ; my baby suffering for food and for shelter ! and she was *begging !* I see *that* too ! "

Immediately my thoughts flew to the mother, and the condition I had found her in, when taken home by the child ; the recumbent figure in the corner, the tawdry finery hanging around, and the proof I received from the woman's own lips of the business she was engaged in. I was not in the least surprised that he should follow me here ; and I trembled in every limb, as he inquired, still with those eager eyes looking into my soul,—

" Where was Mary, then ? "

" At home, sir," I replied, determined that this time I would insist upon that soul of mine keeping one secret, and I felt that this was not the time or place for full particulars.

CHAPTER XVII.

THERE has not been a night since Mary left me, but I have dreamed of her and my little one. So tall"—and the man stretched out his hand as if in spirit he already covered her precious head. "Mary told you, I suppose, about my other babe? She died five years ago, and"—here the low tones ceased entirely, and again, for a moment, the storm of sorrow swept over his head—"since then I have been utterly adrift."

I longed to ask him about the wife which the laws of the land declared his, but somehow I could not form the necessary sentence. What right had I, I asked myself, to again bring this man and woman together, supposing, as I most certainly did, that the same insurmountable barrier existed which had kept them apart all these years? and then, supposing this first wife no longer lived, what reason had I for thinking that he would so far set aside all previous examples as to marry a fallen woman, even though he was the only one responsible for such downfall? "Have you not gone a trifle too far?" suggested that "still, small voice," which, until now, I had been too excited to notice. "What is going to come out of this? Has Davy Crockett's "Be sure you're right, and then go ahead," had any influence in bringing about this remarkable and partial finale, or have you been swayed by impulse, and impulse alone?" How many times have I heard parents say to children, and friend to friend, "Decide this question entirely by the head. Do not allow your heart to have the least voice in the matter." This then seemed like good counsel; but I have decided since that the opinions which the head without the heart arrives at, or the heart without the head, are diametrically opposed to the logic of Christianity. "But have you not been overwhelmingly governed by heart? Tell me, what has sound common sense, which is the foundation of true reasoning, had to do with the visit to this merchant?" continued the voice tantalizingly, and without more ado I went to work settling the torment. In a second, the head, which had been seemingly ignored in the transaction, came in with a squelcher. "There is no necessity of laying down premises to prove myself correct. Mary and the man before you love each other as fondly as it is possible for man and woman to love. Their affection has stood the test of time and separation; and now it is none of your business whether or no the legal partner still lives, or whether protracted inharmony has resulted in divorce. Your duty lies with the fact that a sister is dying for the love it is in your power to give her. "Shall she ask for bread, and be given a stone?" "But this is not logic!" says the reader. "You confess yourself in favor of a monogamic marriage, and now you are showing that love is the only test that can be applied to such unions! Of a verity, this is a contradiction."

Life is full of contradictions and seeming inconsistencies, my friend; and yet, after all, many are more honest in the expression of different opinions, at different times, on the same subject, than we give them credit for. That laws for the government of humanity are absolutely necessary, no one in the possession of his senses can dispute; but it is not possible for one man, or a set of men, to frame laws which can be made applicable to every case. This merchant had committed a sin against the law when he allowed the flood-tide of love to render him oblivious to that law. Still, this very love, the divinest part of his nature, was, from the very reason of that divinity, a million times purer, and more powerful, than any statute that the brain of mortal can ever frame. Now, this was *head*-work; and as I scanned again the noble features of my companion, went over again the cruel years which had deprived him of all he held dear, the head was reverently bowed — bowed, as it always must be, to the omnipotence of love. I've liked my head better ever since the bringing in of that verdict. It evinced a harmony of feeling and action which argued well for future quandaries.

"What a wretch I have been!" he resumed, after a moment's quiet. "If you would only tell me how I can ever atone for the wrong done Mary and my child, I shall be *so* glad; but there really seems no way. I honestly believed when I took her as my own (God bless the darling! she was my own, *is* my own, cherished as I think few men *can* cherish a woman), that I should be able to keep the manner of my living a profound secret until — well, until — I might as well make a clean breast of it — the wife the law had given me was removed. I had no idea of a divorce; I knew that a separation of that description could never part us, because, demon-like, she would pursue me, and make my life, thus parted, more wretched than ever. Her temper was most violent — entirely uncontrollable. When in one of her terrible fits of passion, which she was at all times subject to, I was compelled to be ever on the defensive, and, in order to save my own life, would often be obliged to hold her hands until the frenzy spent itself, and she would lie back weak and sometimes penitent. It was a species of insanity, I have no doubt, but none the less terrible to bear. This incessant strain upon the nervous system brought about heart disease, which her physician pronounced incurable, and likely at any time to terminate her existence. Just remember, madam, that we had never taken a moment's **real** comfort in each other's society; that, from children, our fathers, from some ridiculous family compact, had determined upon our marriage; and that **these insane** ebullitions of temper had been carefully concealed from us,— and you will be able to form some idea of my position when love, the real, genuine article, came to me. I could not refrain from possessing the dear child, and, to do this, I resorted to subterfuge and occasional falsehood. What would I not give to be able to blot out the dreadful past? But come, is it not time to go? Perhaps my course will be plainer, after having once more confessed my sin and sorrow."

"Then, you have no children living save little Mary?" I queried, hoping to get at other information.

"No, my friend, she is all; God bless the darling! My wife lived just six months after Mary left me, and"—

"What! your wife dead? I interrupted.

Then you are free from all restraint, free from all legal ties, free to do just as your heart. dictates! Thank God!" I almost shrieked, so relieved that I could not help the expression.

"And were you unacquainted with the fact?" he inquired, while a look of perplexity was plainly visible.

"Entirely so," I answered, with a long-drawn sigh of relief.

"But how did you dare approach me if unaware of my liberty? Were you ready to set at defiance the conventionalities of society, and allow love to be heard in this case? or what were your ideas?"

"I think I had no very definite ideas on the subject," I replied. "I knew that Mary was perishing, and that you could do her good; and I came to you, I think, because I couldn't help it. A will stronger than my own sent me. But I am really overjoyed to know that hereafter everything may be carried on without dissimulation." I could not but be struck with the gentleness, as well as the genuine fortitude displayed by my companion. Tears stood in his large dark eyes — tears impossible to hide, yet there was a strange calmness in his manner, which surprised and pleased me. I felt instinctively that I could trust him in the interview which was so soon to take place between him and the woman from whom he had been so long separated.

"Now, if you think best, Mrs. Kirk, we will go," he continued quietly. "I do not think my appearance will attract observation; do you?" and there was in the pleasant tone, so much of friendliness, and real trust in my desire and ability to be of assistance, that my heart grew warmer and my sympathies stronger.

"My friend," said I, rising,— thus expressing my willingness to depart,— "do not, I beg of you, appear surprised at anything you may see in the place to which I shall take you. You have probably never entered a house so miserably squalid in appearance as the house where your Mary is compelled to reside; although she is now provided with every comfort.

"So bad as that?" he queried. "Well! let

us go, or I fear I shall not have strength enough to take me there."

Just then a rap was heard at the door, and without waiting for an invitation to enter, the visitor presented himself. Imagine my surprise when the minister, of whom mention has been made in a preceding chapter, walked briskly in, and with an air of conscious power, made known his business. I had seated myself with my back to the door, but had caught a glimpse of the hypocrite's side face, without recognition on his part, and then waited, with considerable curiosity, I confess, to hear the object of his visit. Oh, how my blood boiled! This wretch, whom the world supposed was entirely engrossed with the saving of souls, but whose special business it was to drag down to the lowest depths of infamy the weak and helpless — the man I had driven from the house of the woman whose God-given husband had just taken the scoundrel by the hand, with all the grace and suavity of a refined gentleman, as well as a sincere disciple of Jesus — made known his benevolent errand.

CHAPTER XVIII.

"I HAVE called, my dear sir," said the wolf, so thoroughly disguised as a sheep that a person unacquainted with his real character must have believed him the dear innocent he represented, "to see if I could interest you in a poor family (I will only detain you a moment) that I have lately had fall upon my hands. A very interesting case, I assure you,— a widow and five children, the eldest only eight years old. I have just returned from the miserable apartments in which they live, and the distress I have been compelled to witness, accustomed as I am to scenes of destitution and wretchedness, has caused my heart to ache bitterly."

"I am very much engaged this afternoon Mr. ——," replied the merchant kindly, "and have not time to talk the matter over; but,

to relieve immediate distress, allow me to give
you a small sum, which will at least keep
the family from starving for a few days;"
and I turned to see a fifty-dollar greenback
just on the point of being transferred to the
minister's long greedy fingers. At that moment I confronted him. Many times in my
life have I waxed wroth and indignant, but
never before did I feel so thoroughly pugi-
listic! I could well understand then how men,
taught, as they are, from infancy, the "manly
art" of self-defence, are ready, when occasion
demands it, to pitch in and make a corporeal
impression where a moral one is not possible.
There was no question but the scamp needed,
as Mrs. Partington would express it, "a good,
sound trouncing;" but all I could do was to
glare with my eyes, and "trounce" with my
tongue, which I declare was never in better
running order.

"Put that money back in your pocket, sir,"
I commanded, more like Xantippe herself than
the modest, self-possessed woman I was desirous
of showing myself. "I would not trust that man

with ten cents; a man who will assist in the downfall of women, who will lie, and creep, and play the part of a seducer and hypocrite through the week and explain the word of God on the Sabbath, will also steal. Give me the residence of that **poor** family whose sorrows you so glowingly picture. Mr. —— and myself are just going out, and we will call there and render all the assistance necessary."

The merchant came to my side, and taking my hand in his, said soothingly and respectfully, —

"But, my dear friend, you have made a mistake; this gentleman is the· Rev. Mr. ——, whose character is above reproach."

"It would be unbecoming a Christian gentleman," said the parson, who had just found breath to speak, "to show any anger in replying; yet I feel that there is, as the just and glorious Paul expresses it, such a sentiment as righteous indignation. This female," with an accent on female, which, under other circumstances, would have been ludicrous to the last degree, "I have never, in my life, laid eyes on until this moment, and I defy her, or any one else, to produce an incident in my life which shall reflect to my discredit."

"If you can trust me in other matters, sir," I replied, addressing my companion, who still stood close by my side, "you may trust me in this. A short time ago, a poor woman, whose life had been cursed by disappointment and"—

"I shall be compelled to bid you good afternoon, sir" interrupted the clerical cheat, making for the door. "I will call again, when sure of finding you alone. Your visitor is evidently an excellent candidate for Bloomingdale. I cannot remain without losing my temper, although aware that the woman labors under the strangest hallucination possible to conceive of."

"You will go, sir," said I, "when I have finished, and not until then," and placing myself against the door, effectually barred his egress. "As I said before, a woman who had been driven to desperation by the bitterest disappointment, who was unable to procure by honest labor the commonest necessaries of life, broken down with her weight of woe, appealed to this man for spiritual comfort. He talked to her a little while of Jesus, of the wonderful love and wisdom of God in thus proving his boundless affection by the great test of chastisement, and then volunteered to call on her. She gave him permission, hoping there might be something in the religion of which he was a popular representative, to cheer and console. One visit served to demonstrate the fact that her spiritual adviser merely sought his own lustful gratification. You may well look astonished; but this is the literal truth; and if my word is not sufficient, I am prepared to prove it."

The merchant's face was ashen pale. I could see that he had a suspicion of the truth. "His intended victim was not—was not"——, he inquired, almost in a whisper.

I shot him a glance, which he interpreted aright, and continued: "I do not believe he can give the residence of any such family as he has described; not that there are not hundreds of such in our midst; but the poor and needy are among the least of his troubles. Your minister simply desired an addition to his pocket-money for some anticipated sub-rosa, anti-orthodox *spree*. You are at liberty to leave now as quickly as you please."

"You will live long enough to repent this, I trust," roared the parson, making a hasty and undignified exit.

"How much money has that fellow fleeced you out of, I wonder?" I could not help asking, as the merchant contemplated the door, from whence had issued this clerical humbug.

"Is it possible that I have been imposed upon all this time?" he replied. "I really can make no estimate of the amounts I have given the man from time to time; thousands of dollars, probably; and, no doubt, every shilling has been transferred to the man's own pocket. Tell me, Mrs. Kirk, where did you first make the discovery in regard to his real character?" And the sad eyes took on a sadder look, as he waited for me to answer.

"Oh! never mind where, just now," I re-

plied, evasively; "I will entertain you **some**
time with an account of a **few of** my experiences; and now let us go before we are again
interrupted."

"Something told me, my friend," he continued, without withdrawing his gaze, "that my
Mary was the woman you have reference to.
If it is so, tell me; and, by Heaven, I'll find
a way to make the wretch wish he had never
been born. Tell me now! It is my right to
know."

Aye, thought I, how many terrible things you
had yet to learn, my dear sir! How are you
to bear the disclosures which must be made?
Would it not be well to keep the past a secret?
Why is it necessary to harrow up the man's soul
with an account **of** the manner in which his
Mary had kept herself and child from starving
during the long years he had been separated
from her? Surely, Mary would never tell him,
and I was morally certain I never should.
Would the man grasp the whole truth by his
keen intuitions? And then again, wasn't there
another side to the picture? Had he any right

to inquire how she had supported herself, so long
as he had been the cause of her hand-to-hand
struggle with the agonizing realities of life ?
And then, again, there was poor, weak human
nature, there were the rules and requirements of
established conventionalisms which say to a man:
"We will wink at whatever sin you may commit.
It is not very pretty, perhaps; but, then, bad
women are necessary evils;" and to the woman,
"Get thee behind me, Satan! The very sight of
you is contamination." I weighed all these,
and pitied my companion more than ever. Men
are taught from childhood to expect so much
more from their mothers, sisters, and lady friends
than ever comes into the head of a woman to
demand from the opposite sex, that it is no
wonder that many men are unreasonable in their
expectations, and despotic in their government.
The whole social puzzle seemed unravelled then,
and it has ever since appeared very singular to
me that women who have had opportunities for
cultivation and mental and spiritual growth, are
not awake to the fact that a woman should be
held in no more disrespect for ministering to a

man's pleasure or necessity than the man himself. It always did seem to me an even thing; and yet, in common with the rest of my sex, I find that I have often entertained the seducer, and turned a cold shoulder to the seduced, for which my conscience reproaches me bitterly.

"I am overwehelmed with the disclosures of the day," the merchant resumed. "I knew that the world was full of hypocrites; but I had no idea that a man occupying the high position he does, would dare to commit such crimes against society. Don't look at me so reproachfully," he continued, after a brief scanning of my countenance. "I know what you thought that moment. This was it: How dare he make comparisons? Did he not deceive a good woman, and by this deception entail woe and disgrace upon her? I tell you, madam," and the pale face blanched to an ashen whiteness, "I will not allow you to think of that rascal and myself at the same time. I sinned from love and he from lust. Do you not see the difference?"

"I should think, my friend, that you might be aware, from the great difference in my manner

towards you and the rascal who has just departed, of my real feelings, even if I had not expressed as much in language. You have my
heartiest, my most earnest sympathy; and now
let us go."

"I beg your pardon a thousand times, my
friend, for my hasty language. What business
have I, after all, to excuse myself; I who have
doomed to poverty and ignominy my heart's
choice, and my own flesh and blood? It ill becomes me to talk about others! And yet, my
contempt for the wretch who has just left us is
every bit as profound as if I had never been
guilty of sin. One of the inconsistencies of
poor human nature, I presume. You said, let us
go. Yes, let us go quickly. There is not a moment to be lost. What have we been dallying
here for, when my poor little ones are ill and in
danger? Oh! good God! just to think of it;
all these years starving and I rolling in luxury.
Why did she run from me? I could, at least,
have provided her with physical comforts.
Come now, I will order the carriage, and we will
go. Give me some idea of how I am to find

them, or I fear I shall not be able to control myself."

"Please do not disappoint me," I replied, hoping to calm the almost insane man, by appealing to his pride. "I have felt all along that I could rely upon you most implicitly. Your dear ones are comfortably provided for; but the locality in which they have been compelled to reside, as I told you before, is a wretched one; but you must not think of surroundings. Your every energy must be bent toward the accomplishment of a great purpose, namely, the future happiness of the woman and child who have been kept in the mire of poverty and anguish by the great mistake made by you in misrepresenting your real social position. You see, my dear sir, everything comes directly back to you. And if you are not wonderfully discreet and self-poised, I cannot be answerable for consequences."

"Oh! you may trust me; I will be good; indeed I will. You shall never have a word of fault to find. I will redeem the past with the glory of my future."

There was a childish pathos about the voice,

and an indescribably earnest expression of the fine mouth, that brought me again to the realization of the fact that a woman with more knowledge of the world than Mary possessed, when, immature and unsophisticated, he ran with her from her father's house, would have been quite excusable for allowing her heart to greet him quickly.

"See if I don't," he continued. "Indeed you may always trust me. Come," and drawing my arm through his we went down the street into the carriage, and rolled away towards the miserable tenement. "Mulberry street, did you say?" almost groaned my companion.

CHAPTER XIX

OH! this tedious, dreadful groping; this wearisome seeking of the soul for light; this desire to find some clue to the strange entanglement— some thread that will finally lead out of the snarl! May not one be pardoned for honest doubt, even by those who stand firmest in the faith of a merciful God and a glorious hereafter?

Can such things be, and overcome us, like a summer's cloud, without our special wonder? Every revolution of the wheels was taking us nearer to Mary. How would she stand the meeting? How did I dare to take so much responsibility upon myself? If the All-wise and All-merciful had desired, could He not have brought happiness to this strangely-led, strangely-chastened husband and wife, without *my* interference? What was the need of keeping these two souls apart which love had seemingly joined and sanctified ? Was it wicked (yes, I suppose it was; but I couldn't help it, any more than I could keep back the tears that would roll out of my eyes each time I looked at the poor fellow by my side) to wonder what *I* should have done had I been the ruler of the universe? They would have been my children !

Motherly love immediately flew over to Brooklyn, where my own sunny-haired darlings were, and as imagination conjured up a vision of myself, rod in hand, pelting remorselessly into my own flesh and blood, just because I loved them, I grew hard and sceptical and out of patience; and the conclusion was forced upon me, that the world would consider such a mother anything but loving and motherly. I reviewed my own troubles. I tell you, one can think quickly sometimes; and somehow it came upon me that I had not been consulted in regard to my own manufacture or creation. If I had, with the least knowledge of life's bitterness, I should most respectfully have declined the honor. So would, probably, the man by my side; so would most everybody. "That train of thought," exclaims the pious reader, "is not a very profitable one." Perhaps not; but I should like to inquire of my pious friend, what one's common sense or reasoning faculties were given one for, if not to use? and how, in the name of that common sense, a man or a woman can be satisfied with continued castigation? How a loving heart, longing for love, the exquisite essence of life; longing for appreciation, for sympathy, for love's complete environment, — can be made to have patience with misconstruction, separation, and the lack of everything that soul demands for healthy development? My companion was in dead earnest, so was Mary, so was I; and yet the cup of sorrow had been drained to the last and bitterest dregs by each one of us.

"My God! what is all this for?" I could not help exclaiming, though bitterly against my will.

"For joy, I hope, my dear friend," exclaimed my companion, taking my hand in his, and covering it tenderly with the other palm.

"You have suffered, too; and I have been so

absorbed in my own trouble as not to have noticed it. Sorrow makes one selfish, I think.
The past, with me, will simply resolve itself into
an unpleasant dream, if I am only able to make
amends in future. Don't sob so, my dear child,
don't." And the low tones, so intensely musical,
brought a calm to my soul, which at that moment was doubly blessed.

"Here we are," said I; and in a moment more
the driver reined up in front of the tumble-down
shanty.

"Come back to me in an hour for further
orders," said the merchant, as the coachman
waited. "It is hardly safe to wait here that
length of time."

I could not help wondering at the new tone
which the voice had taken on. I knew there
would be no more breaking down; not that the
conflict was over; but the necessity had arrived
for quick and decisive action — for careful self-
control — and the man was ready for the emer-
gency. We stopped one moment at the foot of
the stairs.

"Well, what are we waiting for?" he asked, calmly.

"I will go in first, and after a little preparation, will give the signal for you to enter."

"As you think best," he replied. "But for the love of mercy, do not be long."

Just think! This man had waited ten long, weary years — ten years of agony and torture indescribable; had groped along hopelessly, without glimmer of light, and now the day had dawned, and there was prospect of that peace which comes from mutual understanding. The goal was near — within reaching distance; but the hard patience, which had previously sustained him, was now quite gone, and in its place had come again that insatiable longing, born of hope, which would not brook an instant's delay.

"Please remember that I understand perfectly how you feel, and will be as expeditious as I think prudent. May the Lord grant that the step I have taken — apparently so impulsively, and so replete with love and good will — may result as you desire."

"Amen," he moaned, with bowed head, and hands convulsively clasped.

Now, perhaps, some one will say that I had no right to supplicate in such a manner. Why not? I craved a boon, and asked my Heavenly Father for it. I desired an especial blessing upon my friends, who, it seemed to me, had earned a blessing. I asked for something I wanted, just the same as I used to ask my own earthly father for the means to aid those who stood in need of comforting, knowing that he was abundantly able and willing to grant my humane requests. What is the use of praying, if one doesn't pray for what one wants? It seems to me that most supplications are at least miserable farces. Ever since I can remember, I have wondered at the style of prayer adopted by most ministers. It has always appeared to me that if God really listened to the twaddle which Sabbath after Sabbath was spun out, and respun, and worked over again, in long-winded descriptions of His especial attributes (just as if a man thought to make himself popular with Deity by playing upon his vanity), that if disgust could be felt by

10

one so wise and loving, there would not be room for any other sensation save that and pity! And then, to ask for a host of things which seem especially desirable, after having explained to the Almighty the immense benefit to be derived from such and such a programme, to end with, in substance, this: "But, oh Lord! this seems to us wisest and best; but it is no matter about it— any way that suits you will please me wonderfully." Now, I don't believe there can be found one man, or one woman, in one thousand, who, if he or she knows calamity is threatening them— death or disgrace staring themselves or loved ones in the face—but will, if they believe at all in prayer, pray with all their might and main to have the trouble averted; and if they end such supplications with, "Not as I will, but as Thou thinkest best," the most are guilty of falsehood, for it is not within the limits of human endurance to be willing to be constantly scourged. I don't believe in praying for a new bonnet, or a new suit of clothes, or a ride, or a journey; but if the soul, which must be a part of God's, desires to be gloriously filled with that love, which all admit to be a direct emanation from Omnipotence, the wisest thing, in my judgment, is to ask for it, to plead for it, *because* one wants it, and end with, " I want it—I want it—and cannot be denied." A child may be very still under keen disappointment—when its father has denied certain things which seemed to the little one eminently just and proper—may be still, because realizing that no effort of the feeble will can avail against the stronger paternal one; but it is the silence of defeat, and sometimes of graceful submission, but never because the child has given up desiring the pleasure its little heart so earnestly yearned for. It isn't honest to say to God, "I am resigned to any trouble you may see proper to afflict me with, even if Christ did say, "Thy will be done."

As I turned from my friend, old Mother Thurston came out of her room, on her way upstairs.

"Oh, my dear!" exclaimed the kind-hearted old woman, "I am *so* glad you have got back; I have been praying for it for the last half-hour."

Good gracious! how my heart throbbed. I
could have taken her into my arms, and hugged
her, rags and all, for just that one little sentence.

"But, Mother Thurston, what did you do
that for?" I inquired, hoping that I had at last
found the right description of faith.

"What *for*, do you ask, honey? Why, that is
a funny question to come from such as you.
Why I asked the Lord to send you straight back,
because I wanted you, sure, and the poor creetur
up stairs needed you, of course."

There it was. She had asked for what she
wanted; and I don't believe it occurred to her
to end with, "Never mind about it; it's all
the same to me."

"I told her you'd be here afore long. You
see I somehow knowed it. She has been dreadful kind of anxious about something, and has
ee'n amost strained her big eyes out of her head
watching the door. I couldn't get a word out of
her, no how."

"Well, my dear, you see I am back again," I

said, catching the brilliant eye of the invalid as I opened the door.

"I hope you are feeling better."

"Where have you been?" she asked, almost under her breath, drawing my head down on the pillow beside her.

"Oh! just to make a call," I answered, evasively.

"I am so glad, and so sorry; I hoped, and I was afraid. You know what you said when you went out. Well, I was frightened, because you know he could never forgive me and love me as he used; and I would much rather die than be pitied; but oh, my Father! I could forgive him anything, no matter what it was—could love him if he had committed the unpardonable sin."

"What do you call the unpardonoble sin, my dear?" I interrupted, purposely.

"Oh! I don't know," she replied, dreamily, but"—

"The unpardonable sin, my child, with him, would be his failure to love you as formerly; his determination not to overlook a past for which he is greatly responsible; but I don't think I should say but little of that past just now, Mary."

Oh! how she glared at me. "Some things may safely be left to be inferred, temporarily, at least," I continued, taking no notice of her flashing eyes. "It is better they should be."

"Tell me now, have you? Oh, no, you would not be so cruel. You would never dare take advantage of an accident. I never told you his name—would have died before such disgrace should have been brought upon him."

"What does mother mean by disgrace?" inquired little Mary, advancing to the bedside, and taking the thin, white hand of her mother in hers.

"It seems to me (of course, I don't know much about it), but it seems to me a dreadful disgrace for a little girl not to have any father she can call so, and yet have a father living. Auntie Kirk, I have prayed ever since you went, every minute of the time, to the Lord God, that if my mother's—" and here the little girl hesitated for the right word, and finished with — "my mother's love, and my father was living, you would find him; and if you haven't, *I* shall. I'm not going to bear such nonsense as this much longer, I can tell you." And a look of determination, almost of defiance, transformed the child's face into that of a stern, inflexible woman.

"I don't suppose he's much to brag about, anyhow; but it's a good thing to get acquainted with one's relations, especially one's father. I know who he is now, and where to find him; and if killed for it the next minute, I'll make him understand t'other from which. I don't like sickness, and sorrow, and tears, and rags, and a nasty old house in Mulberry street, and an empty stomach, and cold feet, and no good shoes, and no nothing generally; and then, there is something here," laying her little hand on her heart, an angelic expression taking the place of the late defiant one; "there is something here that wants somebody, something I never had — that isn't clothes or victuals — something to love me — fit to kill me — and if it isn't my father, who in the world should it be? But I wouldn't speak to him if he should walk into this room now — until — well until." Here the tears commenced to flow. "Pshaw! what's the matter with me?" she continued. "I'm almost as bad as mother! What was I saying?" and the pearly drops came **faster**. "Oh! that I wouldn't speak to him until — well, until he told me that he loved me — that's when! What a goose I am! I remember what you told me, Auntie Kirk — that you didn't believe he was so dreadful much to blame. I have been thinking of it ever since. That is the only real good thing that ever was said to me in my whole life! Bless his old heart!"

I knew that the "mother's love," and the child's father was drinking in every word, for I had purposely left the door ajar.

CHAPTER XX.

OH! how that child tortures me! **Mary,** you will drive me mad! Surely, my punishment is greater than I can bear!" murmured the sufferer, turning her face to the wall.

"What **are you always** talking about punishment for, mother? Didn't **you** love my father? say—**now** please **tell** me? **Do** you not love him n**o**w? Have you not *always* loved him? You don't speak. God is love, is he not? He made the love, didn't He? If He didn't know that you and my father were going to love each **other, and** that I should come into this abominable **old world, I** am right sure He didn't know **much, and** what's the use of **talking** about it? It's all plain enough; when you come to think, just right. There is either somebody who fixes things as

(153)

they ought to be, else there isn't, that's all; and what's the sense of fretting either way?"

"That is very strange talk for a little girl," said the invalid, forgetful for a moment of the agony she was enduring.

"I know it, mother. I know it, Auntie Kirk. I just feel that I am nothing but a little girl; but I have had plenty of time to *think*, and I have done it, too. I couldn't have come here without the Lord willed it so. I am one more, just a little speck more, that is all; but if He has counted the hairs in everybody's head, it wouldn't be fair to leave mine out; and just please tell me how in the world I could be here if God didn't desire it so? And now—(I only wish I knew how to talk. I will one of these days, see if I don't)," and the dark, beautiful eyes, so luminous with intelligence and that winsome spirituality, which was the darling's greatest attraction, became so magnetically fascinating, that both her mother and myself were spell-bound for the instant. "And now," she continued, "He must have known all about who was to be my mother

and father; and I shouldn't have been myself at all if it hadn't been so—do you see?
And if God fixed it that way, it must be
right, and there is no sort of use in crying
over it. *I* shall go to my father, if you haven't
got ahead of me, Auntie. I see something
strange in your eyes, Auntie. Mother, look!
Don't you see it too? Oh! you have. I know
you have. Mother, are you blind? I *have*
got a father, and that father loves me; and
mother, you have **got a** love, and that love
loves you; and he has always loved you; and
I can be kissed; and I can be hugged, and
called beautiful names; and I can have all
the clean stockings I want, and buttoned gai-
ters, just big enough, and nice dresses; and
mother needn't cry any more; and she can be
kissed, and have a nice house to live in. Oh,
Father in Heaven!" and **here** the distracted
child threw herself upon her knees. "Oh,
Father in Heaven! what a dear, kind, good,
splendid Father, to have waited all this time
until this little girl has grown big enough to
know what comfort is; because, dear Father,

if she had always had what she wanted, she would never have known how good it was. Please be very loving to Auntie Kirk for making me believe that it would all come out right one of these days; because the feeling that there was nobody in heaven to care for me, was ten million times worse than an empty stomach, and no stockings and shoes. Make mother see it, too. Oh, wont it be jolly, when my own papa comes and folds us close to his heart? and it will be you that sent him. You, oh, dear, good Heavenly Father, who gave us all trouble that we might taste ease of comfort. Give Auntie somebody to love her, too; somebody that will make her heart sing all day, and be glad every minute. Change the sad light in her eyes to one so full of joy and gladness that everybody who meets her will know her heart is filled up to the very tip top, and hasn't room for a bit more. Please, God, don't send us any more tears; because we have all cried as much as we need, and have got enough of it. Make mother as glad as I am that we have had sorrow and trouble, but for all our sakes, and Jesus Christ's sake, send mother's love to us quickly."

"Amen," responded the invalid, now as calm as a child upon its mother's breast.

"Amen," I sobbed, with my eyes fixed upon the door.

"Amen," came in deep, sonorous tones from the husband and father, who just then came slowly into the apartment. Mary, with her eyes closed, drinking in the full inspiration of the little one's prayer, did not first notice the visitor, but the child, just rising from her knees, caught the first glimpse of her father.

With an enraptured cry of "Papa!"—a cry in which there was no feeling but of joy bliss, and love unutterable; a cry so full of angelic affection that it rings in my ears still—then with a mighty effort drew back, saying,—

"Not me first. Oh, not me first! Mother, here's your love. Oh, what a splendid God that was to answer my prayer so soon! I never will doubt him again."

"My *love*," faintly whispered Mary, slowly

turning her head toward him. " *What* do you say, my *love*, my *darling?*"

Their eyes met. So far, the merchant had not spoken a word.

" Oh, no; it can't be; but I thought I saw him then. I think I must be dying. Mary, come here. I am going — go — " and the weary lids closed, and the feeble breath seemed to cease entirely.

" Mary, my love, my darling, my angel, speak to me! I am here. Your own precious husband. Open your eyes. God is good, darling. We shall never be parted again." And in a second more the limp figure was in his arms. Up and down the seven-by-nine apartment he walked, pressing kiss after kiss upon cheek, lip, and eye, calling her by the most endearing epithets. Oh! that the whole world could have seen that reunion. I don't care how straight-laced or orthodox or conventional they might have been, every other feeling would have been swallowed up in the one glorious idea of love.

" She has fainted," I ventured to suggest. " Would it not be well to bathe her head and face with cold water?" fearful that he would extinguish altogether the little spark of life remaining.

"Do not be alarmed," he replied. "She is reviving. Joy seldom kills, you know." And, sure enough, as he spoke, the trembling lids unclosed, and the recognition was complete. The first words she uttered were,—

"Charles, am I dreaming? or am I in heaven? But then you don't know all. Oh, dearest' what sent you back to me? You can never forgive me."

"Mary!" and the merchant laid the invalid back upon her pillows. "Mary, my own precious wife, I implore that you will consider me wholly responsible for the past, whatever that past may have been, and please never revert to it again. I am free from all legal ties, and you shall be mine in a few moments by human law, as you have always been by the divine. When you are stronger, I will make many things plain to you ; and now, my *daughter*."

The child's face was as pale as death; but

with a joyful cry she bounded into his arms, and hid her head in his neck.

"All I could have asked," he murmured. "As sweet and as beautiful as the heart of a parent could desire."

"What long whiskers; and how black they are; and what big eyes you have got, papa; and how much they are like mine, and mother's; and how handsome you are; and oh, dear Heavenly Father! how much I love him; *but, papa, what a long time you have been coming.*"

This was more than the strong man could bear.

"Yes, darling," he replied. "But I have sought you day and night, until my heart was almost broken." And then he burst into tears.

"Oh, don't, papa! please don't! No more tears now. God has fixed it all right. If it had come before, we shouldn't have been half so happy. Let's be good."

In a moment more, Mary had tottered out of bed, and drawing her husband's hand into her bosom, kissed away the tears, and the strong arm gathered her once more to her resting-place.

There they sat, one on each knee, sheltered and content.

"Oh! Mrs. Kirk," said the merchant, a bright smile breaking over his handsome features, "I wish I had another arm to offer you."

"I wish you had," I murmured, through blinding tears; for to save my life, I could not help a sort of "out-in-the-cold" feeling which was anything but agreeable.

"Next to my wife and child, shall I always cherish you, if you will let me." And as cherish had a very pleasant and protective sound about it, extremely soothing to the tired soul, I gave him both my hands on "cherish," and this is about all. An hour after, the invalid was removed to the——Hotel, a minister summoned, and the nuptial knot tied; and now they are at home, where, dear reader, I trust your blessing will follow them.

11

A SEQUEL TO "UP BROADWAY."

"Life is too short for logic.   What I do
 I must do simply.   God alone must judge,
     For God alone shall guide.
 I have snapped opinion's chains, and now I'll soar
 Up to the blazing sunlight, and be free."

KINGSLEY.

A SEQUEL TO "UP BROADWAY."

CHAPTER I.

"TOO short for logic!" Ay, too short! So let us now for a while shut our eyes upon syllogisms, formalities, established conventionalisms, and legal penumbra, allowing heart and common-sense to utter a few words of truth and soberness.

"What could have induced you to give 'Up Broadway' to the world?" is an inquiry which has been made thousands of times since its publication. "I cannot conceive how you dared tell such a story." "The world is not ready for such fearless exposition of sentiment." "Some things will not bear ventilating, and 'Up Broadway' tends to immorality." "It is simply impossible for a woman who has once sinned, as did the heroine of your story, to be possessed of any purity of thought." "A man is a fool to trust a woman under such circumstances," etc.

The above are just a few quotations from the scores of letters I have received in reference to "Up Broadway." The amusing part of the business is that not one of these critical effusions fails to end without an inquiry as to my heroine's whereabouts, how she can be best approached; in many instances requesting letters of introduction. Does this not tell a wonderful story? Does it not plainly demonstrate that, under this thick crust of conservatism, which must of a necessity beget a vision shortened and distorted, there lies a kindliness and nobility of purpose which needs only a few mental earthquakes to shock into action. Occasionally these dreamers are startled from their lethargy by an account of some tragic affair, which for a moment sends the righteous blood in active circulation. Then they stop to think and ask what these things mean, and are often tempted into the expression of opinions which, not unfrequently, frighten themselves. The last on the list of horrors was the murder of Albert D. Richardson by McFarland; a man who, for love's sake, was most foully murdered, and who as surely died a martyr to popular ignorance and bigotry as Stephen Polycarp, John Brown, or Lincoln. So we go. Richardson is not canonized yet; therefore, **every venerable** constitutional conservative, from the Pope at Rome to the King of the New York gambling hell, is busy hurling at him the greater anathema; and every obscure little dog connected with the press joins in the chorus of howls: and the smaller and filthier the animal, the louder his squeak on this especial topic; the nobler and purer the men who have defended the martyr, the intenser the delight with which these curs strive to tread them under foot. Some of these puppies may grow to be big dogs yet. Who knows? But the majority, we fear, will waddle down to their graves growling and snarling, unmourned and unhonored save by their own mongrel brotherhood.

"Why did Eleanor Kirk **write** 'Up Broadway'?"

I will tell you, my poor, fettered, scared-to-death friends: First, because "Up Broadway" is a faithful history of events which actually took place,—a wonderful one in some respects, I admit, but as true as the sunlight. Secondly, because I felt it to be a duty, a most imperative duty, that I owed to the thousands of women, who, through cold and hunger, heart and soul starvation, have been driven to desperation and prostitution, to show them what one woman, by the aid of kindness and rightly-directed sympathy, has been able to accomplish. Thirdly, because I felt that the world needed just such a history, and it was high time that these one-sided, straight-laced, unforgiving, canting members of society should thoroughly understand that another than Christ had for love's sweet sake forgiven a woman! And lastly, because my soul reaches longingly out not only toward the oppressed and down-trodden of my own sex, but to all those who are bound by the fetters of an unloved, uncongenial matrimonial alliance. Although women may be, and undoubtedly are, by reason of larger sensitiveness and less physical force, the greater sufferers from such unions, yet it is the height of folly to predicate that women only are made miserable by this non-conformity of affection and natural temperament. I know of women to-day whom an angel from Heaven could not live with in peace and harmony, and would probably not try after one day's experience, because, let us hope, that with the higher light and knowledge which men must attain to in another state of existence, they understand that which it would be well for many poor, unhappy, struggling wretches to understand on earth,— that a marriage without love is no marriage at all. I realize to what I am exposing myself. "An advocate of free love!" I hear some of you say. "Yes, sir; yes, madam; free love! Not according to your definition of the term, however. Love, the genuine article, the divine, earnest, glorious affection which makes men and women willing to be scouted at, despised, injured, maimed, and martyred for its precious sake, is always free. Fetter it if you can; imprison it, and it will gush out from between every bar, and make the earth glad with its melody.

I abhor and turn my back upon the lust and

licentiousness which characterize the devotees of this comparatively new doctrine. What do men and women know of love who have no wish or thought beyond the gratification of their sensual desires? What do worms and toads understand of the glory of God's universe? Still we cannot help seeing, although we admit it with pain, that this immoral state of the community is chiefly attributable to the fearful amount of prostitution in marriage. In other words, men and women, tiring of each other, discovering too late to be of service that there is no bond of sympathy between them, realizing that the law cannot interfere in such cases, start out in pursuit of something which they are unable to find at home. Many, it is true, wear these fetters meekly, making no attempt to escape, either righteously or otherwise, from the thraldom of an unloved, unhappy marriage relation. Not a few believe it their duty to stay and suffer, and so sacrifice health, comfort, and everything which makes life endurable, to a morbid, and, when rightly viewed and analyzed, a wicked observance of a law which it seems to me could never have been framed for the intelligent, intellectual nineteenth century.

"I do not love him; he is unkind to me; he never consults my wishes; I loathe the very idea of being brought in close personal contact with him: what shall I do?" asks more than one woman in New York to-day.

"Why, leave him; allow him to go his way in peace; you go yours."

"But the laws of the State will not allow me a divorce for unkindness, or brutal treatment even. I am not prepared to prove that my husband is untrue to me."

"Exactly, my dear; but that does not alter your duty. Women, strangely enough, seem to have imbibed an idea that when they are tamely submitting to neglect and abuse, to fault-finding, and blows perhaps, that they are doing God service; that because, according to a ridiculous statute which insists that the two joined together by priest, minister, or justice of the peace, God has united, they must consequently endure every species of indignity which either or both desire to inflict. What a grand thing it will be for humanity when men and women learn that no men or set of men, no law or set of laws, can bind soul to soul, and that neither powers or principalities, things above, or things below, are able to separate soul *from* soul. Will some one explain why it is a woman's duty to live with a man who abuses or ignores her? why it is a man's duty to remain under the same roof with a woman he abhors? Who says you shall lie prostrate, and allow this man to tread upon every sentiment of right, every noble inspiration and impulse? Who says you shall take without a murmur every description of abuse and contumely? Who says you shall submit to his fiendish caresses, and bear his children? Who says you can be knocked down and dragged out, your little ones taught every imaginable wickedness? Who says convict your husband or wife of adultery, no matter how it is accomplished; employ a friend or detective to lead them into the haunts of vice, or inveigle them into suspicious positions, we will wink at the *modus operandi*, but we have no desire and no power to separate what God has joined together for any of the above minor causes? I will tell you: The laws of the State of New York.

Do you still ask why Eleanor Kirk wrote "Up Broadway"? Once more: To give men and women courage; to show them, by the recital of a true story, that love is mighty, love is omnipotent; and to do away, as far as possible, with the old-established idea that marriage, by priest or minister, is a God-ordained rite. In the "Sequel" she hopes to convince a few, at least, that one kind of suicide is as wicked as another, and that no human being has a right to throw away or tread upon his or her happiness, thereby making miserable and shortening the lives which God has given. The number of women who have gone down to their graves broken-hearted is fearful to contemplate; and men *have* been found foolish enough to stay and be made miserable by heartless and wicked partners. Still, men are not fettered by the same laws which bind women. A man, failing to find peace and comfort at home, can spend his leisure hours at club, lodge, or with the woman or women whose society he prefers to his legally-made wife. The world knows of this, winks at it, believes in it, and pities the poor fellow who is so terribly henpecked; and he is received with open arms in any society he chooses to enter. Now let us reverse this. What if the wife, disappointed and uncomfortable, attempts to solace herself with others—what then? Why, she is an outcast and a reprobate at once, and anathemas both loud and deep are hurled at the suffering woman. For my own part, I wage no war against this treatment of so-called wives by Mrs. Grundy. On the contrary, I am glad of it, and consider it eminently healthy, but fail to understand why husbands are not subjected to the same social treatment. While the relations of husband and wife are sustained by the parties bound, neither party has the least moral right to seek solace and entertainment in the society of the opposite sex. Both honor and common decency forbid it. It is only when such relations have entirely ceased —when the husband and wife, after careful and conscientious effort, discover that harmony is a condition unattainable, having previously given

fair warning of his or her determination to quit
forever, that the question of happiness from
another **quarter** should be considered **for** a
moment. **Then** comes the God-given right **to**
seek comfort, **if it** is not already within reach.
Do not misunderstand or misconstrue, I pray. I
only wish to convey the idea that it **is** the duty of
every, human being to be happy, when this
happiness does not conflict with or mar the comfort of another. The man who lives in husband-
ly relations with the wife the law has given him,
must be entirely devoid of every manly attribute
when he enters into **such relations** with another.
No man can be true to two women, no woman to
two men. This is entirely out of nature, and
those who thus deliberately set aside morality,
and decency deserve all the ignominy such
behavior is sure to entail, and all the contumely
the world can pile upon them.

"I have children: what shall **I do?** said a
legally-made wife to me the other day.

"Do you love the father **of** those children?" I
inquired.

"*Love* him? No!" she replied. Neither does

he love *me*. Sometimes there are whole weeks that we do not speak together even; then again he will be quite pleasant for a day or two. He is not only unkind to me, but I know he loves another. Until I discovered this, no woman ever tried more faithfully than I to please a husband; but it was no use. I am a good housekeeper and a good mother; but I have no way to earn my living. I don't know how to do anything except to take care of my family. What *is* there in the world for me?"

Such as these are hard cases, but there can be but one answer: "Take your children, if you can get them, and march out into the world—anywhere. Place the little ones in the care of friends, or in an asylum, if their father will not contribute to their support, and then go to work at something. Better be a cook, waitress, scullion even, than an adulteress, than the unwilling victim of a man's lust, whose love you know is given to an another."

"But if I remain, my children can be taken care of, educated, and brought to fill positions of which I may be proud."

"True, but do you realize that by remaining you will probably bring more illegitimate children into the world? for as sure as truth is superior to falsehood, virtue to immorality, love to lust, every child who is not an offspring of love is bastard." Look about among your friends, oh ye of little faith, oh ye who have been fettered with false ideas and ridiculous quibbles in reference to love and duty. Count those among your friends whom you believe to be honest in their relations with each other, see if you do not find those whom even you, bound as you are by the world's conventionalisms, believe would be better off apart! No woman owes anything to a man who is unkind or unloving; no man to a woman for whom he finds he has no affection or sympathy—that is, so far as the intimate relations of husband and wife are concerned. If he have sufficient nobility to wish to provide for the future of his legal partner until she shall have found a way to support herself or be taken care of by another, all right, if she feels like accepting such assistance. As the woman has most to lose by such separation, in a pecuniary point of view, it seems to me simply foolish for her to refuse pecuniary aid when offered, as many women have, to my certain knowledge. There are cases of simple uncongeniality, where the parties implicated are too high toned and well bred to quarrel, and where nothing can be brought against either save a non-conformity of taste and affection. The same rule applies to this as to others. The act of conjugality without true conjugal love to inspire it is the meanest, the most despicable act to conceive of. It is a direct sin against God, a violation of His expressed commands. Thank Heaven! men and women are fast waking up to these truths; and the day that prostitution in so-called married life is abandoned, that day will show fewer brazen females on our streets and fewer adulterers. This woman marries for a home and a **maintenance**; this man because the woman is beautiful, accomplished, and sought after by others; or she is rich, and of aristocratic parents. Everything under the sun is brought into matrimony except the very question which legitimately belongs there, the question of fitness, adaptability, soul-fitness and sympathy,— in

other words, love. Many are linked by the law
of whom nothing detrimental can be said. They
are honest, conscientious persons, members of the
same church, perhaps, and yet they do not agree.
They irritate and annoy each other, and two
lives are made more miserable than words can
describe. Neither can understand the reasons
for such disagreement, because both are perfectly
aware of each other's good qualities. Now, this
is easily explained. There are, we know, chemi-
cal properties which no amount of coaxing will
cause to unite. Oil and water, both extremely
useful ingredients, will not mix, though one
should stir forever. So some persons, pure and
unexceptional in character, will not blend for
similar reasons ; and it is the height of folly to
break one's heart in the vain attempt to bring into
congenial relations souls which were never intended to mate. The only argument which present conservatives bring upon this matter, is,
"How is a man or woman going to know when
he or she has found the mate? Many marry, not
only believing that they love, but that the object
of their love is endowed with every imaginable

virtue. After a short married experience they discover their mistake. What then? Shall they leave these partners and try it again? If so, what guarantee can you give that another mistake shall not be made?" The answer to this, it seems to us, must be that there is no such thing as an absolute guarantee possible in any human affairs. To do the best one can is all that is required of poor humanity. That a man and woman stand before a priest, and vow to love, honor, and cherish each other till death, is certainly no guarantee that they will do so. And when this man and woman find, after mutual and conscientious effort, that they are absolutely unable to keep that vow; that, instead of attracting, they repel each other more and more the longer they live together, it is difficult for any reasonable person to understand why they should remain in bondage. Then as to the forming of a second tie. The guarantee against a second mistake must lie with the individuals themselves. In proportion as they have availed themselves of the benefits of experience; in proportion as they are pure, and of matured and cultivated judgment; in proportion as they make conjugal love a part of their religion, and enter into it purely and unselfishly, they will be guaranteed against all failure in love relations. The great fact that **very** few separations take place in the case of those who have married from pure, unbiased choice is the most powerful of all arguments. Most marriages are, to more or less extent, marriages *de convenance.* Ambition and necessity rule women in their choice of husbands far more than love. All the business of this life is experimental. Nothing is absolutely guaranteed; everything must be tried for; and all protestantism is but a slipping off of the guaranteed noose.

Do you still ask why Eleanor Kirk wrote "Up Broadway?" First, because the story was true, and she considered it right to do so, and felt that hosts of struggling women would be awakened to a sense of their terrible positions, and by the simple narrative given strength to conquer. The courage to publish it must have come from above, for that it required a few grains of this extremely useful quality she has no wish to deny. Had she not been on the most intimate terms with a woman who had suffered in her own person every description of abuse and indignity possible to conceive of, she would not probably have been so deeply interested in the woes of others. "A fellow feeling makes us wondrous kind." Not that there was any similarity in the species of suffering, not the slightest; but contact with misery had aroused her most loving sympathies, and, consequently, made her more willing to be of service to the down-trodden. Let Eleanor tell you about this woman, and then see if you wonder that she at last gained strength to cry out against all kinds of intolerance.

Some years ago there lived in a small country town a young woman whose education, moral and intellectual, had been conducted in the most conscientious and loving manner. The utmost liberality was shown by her parents on all subjects—religion, politics, and general ethics; but on the question of marriage and its duties no Roman Catholic bigot could have been more unreasonable and uncharitable than was her father; and in this atmosphere she grew to be a woman, and married. "As you make your

bed, so must you lie" had been so carefully
instilled into the mind of our friend that she
thoroughly realized this union was for life. As
it happened, the man who had selected her for
his partner was a refined, earnest gentleman, and
no cloud arose to dim the light of their pleasant
intercourse. As it happened, I say, for she was
very young, a mere child, and her husband was
some twelve years her senior. What did this
unsophisticated girl understand of the life she
was entering upon? Nothing, of course. Marriage was invested with a sort of *couleur-de-rose*
haze, and, from the manner of her education,
seemed to her the end and aim of every woman's
ambition. Did she love him? do you ask. She
respected him, believed in him; but the depths
of her heart had not been stirred. This affectionate regard could easily pass for the genuine
article, for the young wife was of an impulsive,
demonstrative disposition, and had not attained
to full womanhood—that is, she had not come
to understand the depth and richness of her own
nature. After a short and painful experience,—
for her husband sickened and died,—our friend

was left a widow with two little ones. Then a
father's loving arms were outstretched, and under
the parental roof she and her little ones were
welcomed and cared for until the "Grim Mon-
ster" again presented himself and removed her
sole remaining relative, leaving the daughter
with her two babies and a sister only one year
older than her oldest child as heritage. Then
came the tug of war. How could she best support herself and the children entrusted to her
care? She was a good scholar, competent to
teach music or belles-lettres, and without a particle of false pride concerning labor. So much
grevious trouble had shattered the poor child's
health, and, mentally as well as physically disa-
bled, she cast about her for the means of support.
A few music-scholars were found. This, with
copying music for a distinguished composer,
brought her, with care and economy, sufficient
for the wants of her little family. God only
knows the anguish of that heart. As has already
been said, her parents were extremely liberal on
every subject but that of marriage. She was
the joy of her father's heart, the light of his

eyes, and the atmosphere of her home had always been redolent with that perfect harmony which can only spring from the purest and most unselfish affection. What wonder **that the** world seemed to her a wilderness ? What wonder that her nights were sleepless, and that as she clasped her little sister to her heart, the last fruit of her parents' glorious affection, and surveyed her own two lusty boys, she half-wished that her parents could have taken them all along with them to the land where, we have been taught to believe, there is no anxiety about what we shall eat or wherewithal we shall be clothed ! How could she, her whole time devoted to the bread-and-butter question, find time to train and educate the precious souls thus entrusted to her care! For a while she worked nobly, then came temptation in the form of a man.

"I love you," he said. "I will care for your little ones. My business position is good. I can give you just such a home as you deserve to be mistress of. You shall be my wife, and no care that love can ward off shall come to you or yours."

Two or three months previous to this offer our friend had been steadily and surely failing in health. A physician was consulted, who said, —

"I would not give three cents for your life if you remain here through the coming winter. Change of air, change of scene, and entire freedom from care, will probably restore you. Medicine is of no earthly use."

Another long, wistful look at the poor little ones. She had just commenced to understand the needs of her own soul. She realized that it was in her power to make some one exceedingly happy, and that the right kind of companionship must develop in her qualities which, brought to fruition, would make this world a very heaven. Could this man satisfy the needs of her soul? Could he make this wilderness of hers bud and blossom as the rose? No! That she saw at a glance. Could she respect him? She thought she could. Could she make him a true, earnest wife? Most certainly. Our friend had been too carefully drilled in the moral code to ever be false in action or thought, even, to the man she had promised to obey. That part of her education was perfect, for which **early** training she devoutly thanks God and her parents; but for that other twin-sister doctrine, which made it imperative for her to continue to live with a man who outraged every noble sentiment of her soul, she feels under no obligations. And here, let me say a word to parents. Educate your daughters carefully. Provide them with some trade or profession by which they can earn their own living if circumstances render it necessary. Advise them in regard to their choice of husbands, and then if they marry, charge them by all that is sacred in soul and body to never allow those whom the law calls master to impose upon or in any way abuse. Let them feel that your arms are always ready to clasp them, your loving sympathy awaiting them, and make them comprehend that a woman can be guilty of no greater sin than bringing children into the world whose father she had been made to loathe and despise.

Higher light and intelligence came to the subject of our story through suffering of the most terrible description, and she cannot fail to see that a little judicious training in reference to the duty all of God's creatures owe themselves, as well as others, would have saved her years of misery.

Well, what should the woman do—how choose? Here was sickness, and probably—after a few months' longer wrestle with poverty—death. There was a comfortable home, education and plenty for her little ones, health and strength for herself.

The man, she reasoned, must love her, or he would never wish to marry her with these incumbrances. Perhaps, in time, she might learn to love him. This is just the place where thousands of women totter and fall, and the greatest of all reasons for the wretchedness so many bound by the law experience.

Instruct your daughters, also, in reference to love. Be careful to make them understand the difference between friendship and love. Tell them that a woman may be pleased with

the society of a man, be really very happy
in his company, prefer it to others of the
opposite sex, and yet be not in love with
him. Drill them so carefully in the different
sensations experienced by all women that they
will be quick to analyze and explain. Cause
them, if possible, to understand that true conjugal love springs from a thorough blending
of soul; that it is self-sacrificing, and that the
questions of maintenance, of dollars and cents,
of brown-stone fronts and dashing turnouts,
never enter into it ; that unless they feel
willing to share discomfort, privation, ay, death
even, that they know nothing of the love which
should possess the soul of a wife.

Our friend had no time to lose. She must
choose quickly; so, without the least idea that
she was sinning against her own soul and that
of another, one evening, after a peculiarly distressing day, she placed her hand in her suitor's
and said, "Your home shall be my home;"
and a few weeks after found her his wife.
They took a house in a neighboring city, and
here commenced the trouble of her life. She

soon found that death was no disaster. Her darlings had died, loving and blessing her; their last words had been heavenly benedictions; their kisses and blessings had mingled with her tears, and had taken away half the sting of parting. How many times in her life had she heard those familiar with grief exclaim, "Ah! living trouble is worse than death!" But she had utterly failed to understand its full significance. Now it came over her like a great flood, she bowed her head, saying, "Why did I murmur when God removed my dear ones? How much better would it have been for my children had I kept steadily on and died even, than to have placed them under the influence and in the power of this bad man." She was not a week married before she discovered that her husband's intention was to keep constantly under the effect of liquor; that when the fumes wore off, or were slept off, he was morose, obstinate, and fearfully profane, until he was again replenished. She had made a grand mistake. The man who called her wife had grossly deceived and imposed upon her. What could she do about it? Evidently nothing. Early training forbade it. "As you make your bed, so shall you lie," was all the reply she received, when she questioned her own soul in reference to her terrible position. This irrational saying has been flung quite long enough at those who suffer from an unhappy union, and it is time that sensible persons discovered that the whole argument upon which is based—the idea that because one is decoyed into an unpleasant position, they shall remain and suffer all the misery such position entails—is just as flimsy and illogical as this: "As you make your bed, so shall you lie!" Ridiculous! What woman is there so weak or so foolish who would not, finding she had failed to spread her couch nicely, arise and make it over again? Yes, and keep fixing it until it does suit her! A man finds himself in the presence of a fiend whom he knows has murder in his soul. Shall he have more regard for the madman's bloodthirsty desire than he has for his own life? Does duty demand that he furnish him with a pistol to blow his brains out? A man rents a house:

it is represented perfect in every respect. He lives in it a while and finds **that** the chimneys are out of order, the flues defective, the roof leaky, and the domicile in every respect untenantable. The landlord obstinately refuses to make the premises habitable. What does he do about it? Remain, and have his eyes smoked out, and his children's health destroyed? A fool might fear the consequences of removal, but a sensible man vacates and tries another. Now, marriage is no more binding as a civil contract than is this contract between landlord and tenant. It is plain to those who will open their eyes that no person has the least right to remain in a position of fear or perpetual discomfort.

Our friend discovered this when it was too late to avert the awful consequences.

CHAPTER II.

A YEAR passed; a child was born — another boy. Her two oldest childen were just the right age to carefully note the behavior of their step-father and be influenced by his example. She kept them as much out of the brute's sight as she could, and endeavored by patience and diligent care to counteract any influence he might exert. A thankless task, for a man constantly excited by alcoholic stimulants is a despot of the most overbearing description. Expostulations were entirely unavailing, and after the first year of her married life she never attempted to advise in reference to behavior, business, or the management of children. Such conversations had invariably ended with a disturbance, from the effect of which it was impossible to recover.

Now, look: In the commencement she did

not love him; had persuaded herself that she respected him, and that this esteem would form a foundation upon which could be built sufficient affection to last through her earthly pilgrimage. Mistaken — wofully mistaken! Every woman who marries with such feelings and for such reasons will sooner or later awaken to the sense of her degradation. There is no way of evading it. Through fault-finding, profanity, and every imaginable abuse, this woman plodded along, with not a ray of light to illumine her rugged pathway. She was too proud to impart the terrible particulars of her everyday life, and consequently suffered alone. Did they have visitors, there was nothing too much that this most unnatural husband and father could do to demonstrate his affection for his family; but as soon as the door closed upon their guests he would immediately relapse into his old moods and probably commit some flagrant act of cruelty to pay for this exhibition of tenderness and good nature. So the years passed on. Another little one was born. Dissipation had now come to be felt in business, and, after repeated efforts to reclaim this strangely besotted man, he was finally dismissed from the firm, and found himself without the means of earning a dollar. From bad to worse he then went. Words are powerless to describe his utter fiendishness, his lack of every manly attribute. Night after night the suffering wife watched for his returning footsteps,— sometimes until almost daybreak,—fearing to go to bed lest he might find her asleep and murder her. When he found that nothing he could do or say to her would provoke a reply, he would frighten her about the children. More than once he has torn the sleeping infant from its warm rest in its loving mother's arms, placed it on the marble mantel, and there, for a time which seemed an eternity to the distressed mother, make it remain, struggling and shrieking. If she attempted to go to the child's rescue, as she had on several occasions, the brute would immediately knock her down. After a while baby would be **thrown** upon the bed, with —

" Take your brat; and I'll give him just two minutes to stop his —— howling!"

" A fool to remain and endure such treatment," do you say? Give us your hand: those are my sentiments.

"Better her children should starve."

So I say. But do you not see that she was simply a victim to the idea that a legal marriage is a God-instituted ordinance, instead of the civil contract it most certainly is? " Whom God hath joined together, let not man put asunder," she applied, like many others, to all those who stand up before priest or minister and take upon themselves matrimonial vows, whether true to these vows or not.

The children were not allowed to attend church or Sabbath-schools. Did he find one of them reading, the book was immediately burned. The "Sunday Mercury" and "Herald" his wife was permitted to peruse; but no magazine, no library book, nothing of a standard character was allowed in the house. In this cruel manner, starved intellectually and socially, this misguided woman performed what she considered to be her duty. Duty? Good heavens! what a misnomer! In the name of all that is good, sensible and reasonable, what did she owe this brute? And what did she not owe herself and children?

"Did she wake up at last?"

Yes; have a little patience, and I will give you full particulars, because I lived with that woman. Another child was born; this time a dear little girl. The pangs of poverty were now keenly felt. There had been no steady occupation since the first grand smash-up. The babe was born in the depth of winter. There was not a particle of wood or coal in the house, and very little to eat. What could be done? She was alone with her children—no one to assist, or be of the least service. She finally sent for a neighbor, and made a clean breast of her terribly poverty-stricken condition. Material for fire was forthwith produced, things made comfortable, a physician sent for, and at ten o'clock the little one was ushered into the world. A few moments previous to its birth the father came in cursing, and, noting the state of affairs, walked deliberately out and was not heard from until hours after. The convalescence from this illness was something remarkable. Without a nurse, dependent upon the kindness of neighbors, she gained steadily and surely, and in a month's time was able to take her place in the family. Without understanding the reason for such a change of sentiment, our friend had been completely revolutionized. Sometimes I have whispered to her that perhaps the difference in gender accomplished this change of feeling ; but she invariably shrugs her shoulders at the suggestion. Be this as it may, the birth of the little girl was the commencement of a new order of things. She no longer cringed and trembled at her husband's approach. He saw the difference, remarked upon it, and was thoroughly mystified. Again she obtained a few music-scholars, and endeavored to assist in maintaining the family. Still the demon alcohol reigned supreme. Never apparently intoxicated enough to stagger, or appear like most men when under the influence of liquor, he was nevertheless thoroughly drunk from one week's end to another. Valuables were sold to satisfy this fiendish appetite, and at last came the grand finale. One morning, after having destroyed a set of shirts she had just finished, on account of some imagined misfit about the neck,—after tearing into shreds the little one's under-garments, locking the door and removing the key the while, so that she should be compelled to remain and witness the destruction,— finding that failed to extort a word of disapprobation, or an ill-natured remark, he seized the sleeping infant from its crib and threatened to dash its brains out against the mantel. With the strength of a maniac she snatched the child from its heartless parent, and defied him; then, entirely overcome with the terrible disgrace of her position, fell upon her knees and implored Divine aid.

"Separate us, O Father!" she cried. "Remove me and mine from the influence of this bad man! Separate us by death, if it seemeth right in Thy sight; if not, place distance between us, and help me in my newly formed resolve to do my duty by myself and my children! Guide and guard, O Father, and give me strength to conquer!"

"Good ——!" exclaimed the brute, as she arose from her knees, full of faith that her prayer would be answered. "Do you feel as bad as that?" and without another word he unlocked the door and left the house. There was a terrible something in her manner which, reckless and fallen as he was, checked further display of brutality, and awed him into a cessation of hostilities. Nothing but utter desperation could have driven her to her knees in his presence, for he had always sneered at every high-toned expression or noble sentiment. She had never dared to speak of God or His attributes, as the least approach to religious subjects would provoke the most fearful language possible to conceive of.

"Your prayer is answered, Nell," said he, coming in late the same afternoon. "I have to-day had an agency offered me, which I have concluded to accept. Will you help me get ready? I shall leave for the West to-morrow afternoon."

Never did woman set about a pleasanter task. She was to receive a sum weekly from her husband's employer sufficient for the comfortable support of her family. Perhaps, she argued, when separated from his bacchanalian companions he may—understanding by bitter experience how difficult it is for a man to obtain a business position after having been ignominiously discharged from a first-class firm—go about his work with a determination to succeed. Still she felt that her position was a very precarious one, and decided that she would endeavor, with the assistance of a few friends, to obtain some employment by which she might earn independence for herself and darlings. She could not afford a servant, and thus the whole care and drudgery of the establishment devolved upon her, weak and trembling from ill-treatment and overexertion. She consulted with her sister, who, young as she was, had graduated from a public school with the highest honors of her class and a scholarship. For this the child had labored indefatigably, and when she discovered the prize was hers her joy knew no bounds.

"It is mine, sister! It is mine!" she exclaimed. "Now I can have a thorough classical education. All you will have to do will be to buy my books and make me presentable."

"It shall be accomplished some way," declared the senior, although she knew it would require almost superhuman exertion on her part. If the salary continued she thought it would be possible to carry out the pet plan, and also to keep her two oldest boys at school, and personally superintend their education; and the end she knew would amply compensate for all the weariness and heart-ache which must inevitably attend a life entirely devoted to the physical and intellectual needs of others. But God she knew would smile on such efforts; and with a heart full of gratitude that her prayer had been answered, and the man whose name she bore removed from herself and children, went bravely to work. Four music-scholars were obtained, the sum derived from such teaching to be devoted to educational purposes. The girl-baby — ten months old — was drilled to take very good care of herself, and while these lessons were going on

sat in her little chair close by, and added many
a delicious tremulant to the solfeggios of
her pupils' instruction-books; while three-year-
old Josey sat in state on the sofa, vaguely understanding that mamma was engaged in something
which required not only her closest attention, but
his best behavior. So the days wore until the so-
called husband and father had been gone two
weeks. Then came a crash which threatened to
completely crush both strength and ambition.
The house agent called. Our friend had been
given to understand that the rent for that month
had been paid. The agent, however, represented
it otherwise, and having had the most disgraceful
experience in reference to payments of this kind,
had no thought of questioning the claim of the
landlord. For some reason, which Nellie could
not for her life understand, he chose to work
himself into a fury exceedingly unbecoming to
a man of his excessively contemptible appearance; for anger is too dignified a passion to be
indulged in by a man without soul. He coolly
informed her that he knew her husband did not
intend to pay the rent, and that he supposed her

intentions were similar; that she undoubtedly had money in her possession, and had better "fork over." The first statement was quite as clear to her as to the intruder. The male occupant of the premises had never intended to settle any bills which had the least reference to the comfort of his family. The other taunts were not at all calculated to soothe the spirit of our rather impetuous friend. She gave him a temperate explanation of the disabilities of the case, and a promise that he should be partly paid the coming week, on the receipt of her weekly allowance. It was of no avail. Finding that he still persisted in his insulting demeanor,—threatening to serve a writ of ejection upon her,—she rose to the level of the occasion, and informed him that possession was nine points of the law; that while she occupied the mansion it was her castle; and that if his own instincts did not serve him to find the door, the aid of a policeman would be invoked. Whereupon he left, but soon returned with an officer, who served the writ upon her without mercy. Here was a situation for a delicate woman, with a baby of ten months old, and

four other children, besides her young sister, to
provide for. A kind neighbor consenting to care
for the babies in her absence, she sallied forth,
strong in mother love, but weak in courage,
to try to find a shelter for those little heads so
precious to her. In vain! Rooms there were
in plenty, but not for women with little
children and without husbands to secure the
payment of the rent. Ay, Nellie was discouraged, and yet her dismay did not prevent
indignation. "Because I am a woman is every
door to be thus shut against me?" she asked
herself. "Have not I hands to labor? Have I
not a willing heart, as well as a man? and cannot these dolts see that there is honest purpose in
my eyes, and intense resolution written in every
line of my face?" Surely any one who had the
least knowledge of physiognomy, either by book-
learning or by natural instinct, could not have
failed to see that there was a spirit in the woman
that the delicate and frail tenement it inhabited
could scarely suffice to hold. Such a one would
not have doubted that she would have died
rather than not do and dare anything for her

babes. It was the eagle with broken wing, indeed, but an eagle still, intent on her eyrie, and never to be content until her eaglets' mouths should be filled and the nest made comfortable. Such a woman can never stop when her maternal duties are done. Winnowing the void air in pursuit of food and shelter had likewise opened her eyes to new views of life, new duties, and new objects of endeavor. She now saw how her own sex was enslaved. Strange, it had never come home to her before. She noted how completely avenues of successful labor were closed to them; how every arrangement of society had reference to their imprisonment in some form or other. Looking at her own arms, chafed with the iron of her own fetters, her eyes were opened to see the same scars on millions of her sisters. The great question of the "rights of women" assumed gigantic proportions, and while travelling from house to house, and agent to agent, her whole heart-aching, soul-harrowing experience passed in review before her. Never before had she given the subject the least consideration. True, she had heard of Miss Anthony, and Mrs. Stanton, and a few others who were laboring for what they termed the emancipation of woman. Old prejudices, early training, a lack of ability to keep up with the times, had, strangely enough, placed the workers in this movement in anything but a favorable light. They had always appeared to her like bold, if not immodest women, and the very idea of a woman's desiring the ballot was quite sufficient to condemn her in the eyes of our friend. Now she plainly saw that simply because she was not a citizen, or, in other words, had not a legal right to live and labor like her brother, she was denied a roof to shelter her children. While waiting at the office of a house agent for the clerk to make out a list of unoccupied rooms, a man stepped up to the desk and inquired for apartments.

"Here you are," said the clerk, mentioning a part of a house which he had just denied her on account of her children. Mortified and annoyed that, simply on account of a difference of sex, this biped by her side, who did not look as if he possessed sufficient vim to take care of himself, could have just what he desired, without being asked a single question, she remarked to the agent,—

"But, sir, you must certainly have forgotten to make any inquiries in reference to the gentleman's family."

"You mean children, I suppose," laughed the agent. "But have you not found out that a man looking for a house with a family of children is a very different affair from a woman in the same situation? You have stated to us that your husband is away from home, and have not said a word about security. This man I know; he has a trade, and I shall have no difficulty in collecting my rent. That's where the rub comes, my dear woman."

"Why hadn't you told me this in the first place," she indignantly made answer, "instead of trying to make me believe my children were the only obstacles?"

"Oh!" replied the smooth-tongued proprietor, "we do prefer to rent these rooms to a man and his wife; but when we are well acquainted with the parties, as in this instance, you can see yourself that it makes all the difference in the world."

Yes, indeed; she plainly saw that there was all the difference in the world between men and women, in pursuit of the same object, and that custom — manufactured by an erroneous idea of a masculine kingship in the world — had placed woman in the condition of a being who could exist only by sufferance in the royal domain of her lord and master.

"What is this marriage?" she asked herself, with bitter inward searching. "Here am I, a woman, with loves, hopes, aspirations, and a sense of growing wings, and a panting after the pure atmosphere of truth and reality. Shams have come to be miasma to my soul; and there is that man,—low, grovelling, sensual; farther from me in spirit than east is from the west; more diverse from me in his tastes and pursuits than is the carrion kite from the eagle,—and behold, he holds the key of my being, and is supposed to lock and unlock at his pleasure the receptacle of my will. He is the arbiter of my destiny, the lawful owner of my body,

14

my soul, my time, my earnings, my children.
He can live with me, and provide for me when
it pleases him; and when his tastes so incline
him he can leave me to seek his own pleasure,
and utterly fail to provide either for me or for
the children I have borne. He can exhaust all
his ingenuity in devising petty cruelties to
inflict on me and mine. He can subject me
to his unnatural lusts, and my babies to his
vile example and teachings. And in all this I
am utterly powerless. The law furnishes me
no escape. There is only one loop-hole of
release from this most horrible slavery, and
that is the possibility of being able to prove
him guilty of adultery — in *flagrante delicto*.
The fact that he is a most gross adulterer, and
has daily sought to debase me and mine to his
own beastly level, does not avail me: the law
has no reference to motives, but only to acts;
and no reference to acts not admissible of the
strictest proof. Two facts stand out pre-emi-
nently: First, I am a woman possessed of no
political rights, and consequently shut out from
all social privileges and remunerative employ-

ment, and on this account denied even a roof to shelter my children; and next, I am a legally-made wife, and the law makes it disgraceful for such a one to take the first step towards freedom."

Cast down, yet not quite in despair,—for in some strange, incomprehensible manner the mere turning over of these questions in her mind had given a force to her will which made fighting a deal easier than it had first appeared,—our friend enters the house that she feels is no longer a shelter for her and her precious ones. What shall she do? The heavens were dark to her; light seemed to have faded out of the sky. Where will she and her children go, when the cruel summons comes to leave their present quarters? She stood looking moodily and carelessly out of the window, as though she were trying to realize that out of doors was all that was left her, and to study the possibility of any comfort, any charity, any hope being able to come to her out of the cold, hard pavement, or the chill November sky.

"Has God forsaken me?" she asked herself; "and is this the fruit I am to reap after my weary planting? Verily, it is Dead Sea fruit, and all the bitterer that my children must eat it as well as I."

But God had not forsaken her. He had yet need of her. A friend and neighbor entered at this juncture—a lady in every way fitted to sympathize with and assist our friend. Warm-hearted and possessed of ample means, she at once volunteered to advance her what was needed to help her out of her present trouble. With this sudden and unexpected lifting of the cloud that had obscured her prospects, came corresponding joy; for she was one of those chameleon natures that take the color of what they feed on; and as hitherto the bitter waters had filled her soul, so now the sweet wine of human sympathy cheered her heart like a medicine. Pressing her babies to her heart, in a transport of renewed hope and joy, she hurried down to the agent with the money which was to secure her another month at least of proprietorship of house and home. No mercenary tyrant would now, for a time at least, dare to question her right to the protection of a roof. Oh! the blessed sense of having a right somewhere to a spot that we could call home,— a right that no other human being can dispute. This sense was Nellie's as now she retraced her steps to her own home,— the home where all her treasures were gathered. But the cup of joy is never unmixed in this world. That very evening our heroine was to discover that the weekly stipend she was to receive from her husband's employer had failed her. The merchant for whom he had gone as commercial traveller informed her that he could pay no more salary until her legal protector (?) should have been heard from, as the latter had valuable samples that might easily be turned to pecuniary account. Nellie, being a reasonable women, could not but see the justice of this, hard as it was for her to accept the consequences. The merchant's conduct was kind and gentlemanly, though, of course, his hopes that she would

get along, etc., seemed rather like the offer
of a fair-looking stone in the place of the
bread she was so much in need of. She had
not yet learned the hard lesson that subsequent contact with the world taught her, — that
while simple justice was a scarce commodity
in society, generosity was still scarcer; and
that a woman, exposing her heart to the sharp
corners of business life, must either suffer or
grow callous. Nothing was heard from the
derelict spouse. Thrown now entirely upon
her own resources, our friend began at once
to call her forces together. The eldest boy
was taken from school and placed in a tea-
broker's office in Wall street; the second, a
mere child, obtained a situation in a store, as
cash-boy. The young sister, whose progress
as a scholar had elicited such high hopes of
ultimate distinction, was also taken from her
studies and obliged to contribute towards the
great work of bread-winning. The music pupils were but few, and the proceeds from that
quarter totally inadequate for the support of
the family. Work of some kind must be

solicited, and that speedily. The first thing done in the needlework line was some embroidery for Lord & Taylor. The young sister applied in answer to an advertisement, and on giving satisfactory references was allowed the privilege of elaborately embroidering a child's heavy piqué cloak and cape, for which, after ten days' steady work, she was allowed the munificent sum of one dollar and seventy-five cents. True, both embroiderers were entirely unskilled, and true that one accustomed to such work could have accomplished it in half the time; but that the compensation was in no way proportionate to the amount of labor, all must perceive who have the least conception of the number of delicate stitches elaborately-made garments of this description require. No more embroidery was of course attempted. Work must be sought, and a kind of work that would fill the children's mouths. With a courageous heart our little friend applied to various families at random. Strange to say, she met with considerable success. Her sweet, earnest expression, so full of honest purpose and determination to succeed, went straight to the hearts of many women, who, engrossed in domestic and social duties, scarcely ever give a thought to the struggling millions crying out for the means of honest livelihood. But oh! who shall tell, as it ought to be told, of the covert insult and suspicion which she was obliged to encounter — of the many snares laid for her tender feet? Does the correct and prosperous and polite world know to what suspicion and insolent advances a young and pretty woman exposes herself, who dares, being poor and hungry, to seek for work? For instance, our friend advertised for shirts to make. Answers to these advertisements were plentiful. Young men called, not with the intention of having shirts made, but with the understanding that the advertisement was a ruse to cover some less respectable proposition. One man called, and, seating himself, very cavalierly began a conversation on the general topics of the day. The advertisement was reverted to by the ladies, but the suggestion was waived by the intruder, and subjects entirely irrelevant to the shirt question at issue discussed very intelligently; for the man was well educated and unusually brilliant. His questions were answered in a quiet and lady-like manner, and then business again reverted to by the hostess. A strange smile played around the villain's handsome mouth as he replied, —

"Shirts, ladies? Shirts? I cannot for the life of me understand why ladies˗ of your elegant appearance should advertise for shirts to make. Some other style of invitation would have answered your purpose just as well, and "——

"And," interrupted the elder sister, rising, "you have evidently entirely mistaken the motives which prompted the insertion of that advertisement. You will have the kindness, sir, to leave the house as quickly as you can make it convenient."

With a muttered curse the scamp left. Having never seen this man before, it might be thought the probabilities were that this would

be the last time the ladies would meet him.
But although in the kaleidoscope changes of this
life of ours the same combinations rarely occur,
it does happen once in a while, by some inscruta-
ble agency, and for some strange purpose, that
the very persons whom one would wish to avoid,
and be unrecognized by, are the ones met.
When, after a little time, our friends, by their
success in the branch of literature they had undertaken, were able once again to enter the
circle of society from which their poverty had
for years debarred them, it was their fortune
frequently to meet this man who had been
ready to insult them in their need. It is needless to say he was what is popularly termed a
"ladies' man;" and though there were more
than whispered surmises afloat of immoralities
which, were society on a really moral basis,
would be sufficient to ostracize the perpetrator
from the pale of every decent family in the
community, he was courted, flattered, and
pampered by almost every woman he met.
Mothers invited the polished rottenness to their
homes, and seated him at their tables by their

daughters, whom, had they been the guilty
partners of his offence, they, the mothers
who bore them, would have doomed to exile
from home, or at least to the utmost social ex-
clusion. He was courted, not as a man, but as a
husband. His great wealth and the appoint-
ments of an elegant establishment were objects
of envy to the opposite sex. These he could
give to the wife whose education had fitted her
for nothing better than the life of a mute bird
in a gilded cage, of a petted slave in a palace.
As a man, he might be vile, reckless, and devilish; as a legalized husband, the union blessed
by the blasphemously misconstrued words of divinity, "Whom God hath joined together let
not man put asunder," he might own and do as
he pleased with the wife who was sold to him.

This is what the laws of the State of New
York and the tone of society bring us to. This
is the effect of that system of education and
misconstruction of Christianity which gives us
two moral codes, one for man and another for
woman, instead of the same law for both.
Not for all the world would I have women

less pure than they are, not for all the world would I have them allowed the license that is given to men; but I would have men obliged to hold their positions by as stern rules as they demand women to live by. I would have them feel under obligations to be as clean and pure as they expect their wives and sisters to be; and, above all, I would have women demand it of them. The majority of women (shame that it should be true) are exacting to the uttermost with women. If a sister slips she must `fall; and fallen, she must be trampled down into the very mud of disgrace and degradation by her own sex, while they smile upon, and perhaps marry, her seducer. Women shut the doors of society against her, and she may walk the streets hellward, even into its very chasm, and be swallowed up by the whirlpool of pollution, while the tempter and partner of her sin is feted and caressed by morally severe matrons, and their daughters, carefully instructed in blandishments, and drilled in arts, are set as baits to trap him into matrimony. None who really understand the working of that moral sham which is known as good society will deny the truth of this statement. Women are educated for but one purpose — marriage. Not for its duties, either, but its position, and what they are taught to regard as its protection. If these fail them, they are left either to a degrading dependence or to a weary struggle for independence against such obstacles as we have cited, and hundreds of others which men, in adopting a career or profession can know nothing of. The morality of our society does not demand that a pure affection should be the motive to this union which it professes to consider so sacred that nothing but death may dissolve it, unless it be the one crime of adultery. It may be policy, it may be lust of the eyes, or lust of the flesh, or the pride of the world that unites the two in this bond. Society and our laws, our church even, demand nothing of the motive so the rite is consummated. Marriage is sacred, says the oracle. As if any form, civil or religious, could consecrate such unions as those we have referred to! Legalize them the "contract" or the priestly benediction may, but make them pure and holy, and free them from being adulterous in the sight of God—never! Yet ordained ministers of the Gospel, anointed priests of the Most High, lend their aid to bind such elements together. Notwithstanding the fiat of the law that marriage is here only a civil contract, and while Mr. Beecher hesitates not to say that he performs the ceremony merely as a civil magistrate, yet prayer and religious rites, even to the benediction allowed by the church only to be pronounced by her ministry, are used when clergymen officiate.

The Rev. Mr. Gallagher, a popular divine in the City of Churches, in an eloquent sermon upon "Our Father," a short time ago, openly avowed that he had joined those together whom God would have had remain asunder, had acted officially at marriages which he knew God neither sanctioned nor approved, and the consequences of which he felt sure would be disastrous. Now, that minister is no exception to the general clerical rule, save in the matter of frankness. Is it not evident to every one that many such mock-

marriges are performed by clergymen every day?
Marriages with which these very reverend gyve-
fasteners know that God has nothing to do. And
if man shall not put asunder what God has joined
together, how shall it be with those whom He
has not joined? Is the disciple above his Master
in this matter? and is the sanction of a man to
outweigh and overrule that of God himself?
For our part we believe what God has joined
together man never can put asunder; and as for
what He has not joined the sooner it is loosed
the better.

But to our story. For two months the wolf
Hunger was kept away from our friend's door,
but the terrible amount of household labor,
together with sewing, music-teaching, and the
demands of a nursing infant, proved too much
for her, and she rapidly failed in health. What
could be done? Everything that human ingenuity could devise had been tried. The old pul-
monary complaint developed itself in a frightful
manner. Sewing dragged. Hope failed. Faith
in God's goodness grew dim. Orders were neg-
lected. What in the world should she do, now

that illness had overtaken her? To whom should she turn? The rent had been punctually paid; now the chances were that she should no longer be able to keep a roof over her children's heads. What would become of her little ones? Only a mother can realize the depth and intensity of this mother's anguish. The pittance brought in by the little boys every Saturday, and the small amount her sister was able to earn, had now to suffice.. This sum would not procure sufficient food for the family, to say nothing of rent, coal, wood, and the thousand and one expenses so necessary to the comfort of a household. "Why don't you write?" had more than once been asked her by friends anxious for her success. "It seems to me you possess the elements of a writer. Why don't you try?" The knowledge that thousands of women in similar circumstances had turned to literature as a last resort, and failed utterly, had deterred her from the attempt; but now in the midst of this wreck, this confusion, this terrible heart-rending suffering, came the knowledge that she must make one more trial before deserting the ship.

Many a time had she, when a child, sat upon her father's knee, after a hard lesson in mathematics, and listened to a favorite song of his, sung on these occasions to comfort the little daughter so dear to him, and give her strength and "spunk," as he facetiously called it, to pursue her studies faithfully. Each verse ended with "Never give up the ship, boys! Never give up the ship!"

The idea of being driven into literature was terribly obnoxious, for she argued that it was impossible for any one smarting from the goading lash of poverty — supposing he or she possessed of sufficient talent — to attain a respectable position among writers. One more trial must she endure before sufficient courage could be given her for the attempt.

It was evening, cold and bleak. A failure to pay the gas-bill had resulted in a removal of the connection pipe, and so, by the light of a solitary candle, she prepared the scanty supper for her family. It consisted of bread and milk. The baby cried for want of proper nourishment, but bread and milk could not be partaken of by the

15

mother if baby starved and died. So weak tea took the place of food, and hot tears rained down upon the little upturned face, whose wondering expression seemed to say, " What have I done that I must be starved in this strange manner ?" So without a murmur — for the children well understood that their mother had strained every nerve to procure them food, and were heart-broken at her miserable appearance — the little ones were tucked into bed. Their innocent petitions ascended to the throne of love and mercy, and childlike. and simple though they were, we believe and know that they were heard and answered, and that speedily. Precious little three-year-old having repeated " Now I lay me down to sleep," &c., and asked God to bless all his relations and acquaintances, ended with this extremely practical entreaty: "Make Josey a good little boy; and please, dear God, send Josey some more milk."

CHAPTER III.

THE mother took the little fellow in her arms, pressed him to her heart, and vowed, then and there, that, in spite of ill-health, in spite of the terrible network of circumstances wound about her, in spite of cold, hunger, and starvation, she would never "give up the ship" until she had reached a place where not only little Josey could have all the milk he desired, but where she herself should be able to say, "I have conquered; I have secured honorable independence for myself and children." Never before had she been so completely bereft, and never before so profoundly certain of success. Go away illness; go away repining. No more time to think of aches and troubles. But what shall she do? Ay, what? "Well, something," she whispered to herself; "and something, too, that will pay." Just then the door-

bell announced that some one—friend or enemy
—desired to enter. Our friend had learned,
from the bitterest experience, that a person to
whom she owed a dollar was an enemy of the
most unrelenting description; and although her
debts were by no means numerous, yet a pull of
the bell was sufficient to throw her into a state
of nervous excitement impossible to describe.
Only those who have had similar experiences can
form the least idea of the soul travail consequent
upon such terrible excitement. An exceedingly
pleasant face met her as she opened the door,
proving to be a gentleman who had visited the
house on several occasions by her husband's invitation.

"I have just heard," said he, "that you were
in great trouble, and have called to express my
sympathy, and see if I could not be of service to
you and your little family."

Her heart almost stopped beating with the joy
of the moment. She knew he was a very wealthy
and influential man; and it was in his power to
do her a great service if he chose; and the kind
expression lighting up the visitor's face gave de-

cided assurance that he intended to assist her in
some way. "Oh!" she thought, "if he will only
help me to a position where I can support myself, I shall soon be able to return the obliga-
tion." After several questions in reference to
her terrible condition, and a few well-timed as-
surances of sympathy, he at last approached the
errand which had brought him to our friend's
house.

"I have come to make you a proposition," he
said. "You must have seen, on the few occasions I have dined at your house, that I not only
admired you very much, but was quite capable
of appreciating a woman of your calibre. I feel
sure that you and I can come to terms without
the least trouble."

"Most likely," replied Nellie ; "for I am willing to do anything which will bring to myself
and family an honorable maintenance. I am
almost distracted with these wretched circumstances and my fearfully unprotected position."

"I understand and appreciate it, madam, and
will protect and care for you with my life if
necessary. You are in delicate health, and quite

unfitted even for the ordinary ups and downs of this strange world. Let me tell you about myself. I have a nice house in —— street, comfortably furnished, and perfectly convenient. I am a married man, I suppose you know," he continued, " but my wife has been an invalid for some years, and on this account my home is not so pleasant as it otherwise would be."

" What could it mean ?" she asked herself. He surely would not invite her to take charge of his establishment. So many children in the house with an invalid would never do, of course, and what could it be ? Her eyes must have expressed wonderment, for he continued still in the same cool, business manner, —

" My dear lady, do not misunderstand me. I will educate your children exactly in accordance with your preferences. Everything, in fact, shall be as you wish it. You will be perfect mistress of your house and of your own actions, and once a week I shall have the pleasure of meeting you."

A strange blindness came over Nellie's perceptions. Looking at him with that vertical corrugation of the brow and diminution of the pupils of the eye which indicate extreme bewilderment, she asked,—

"And why? What am I to do for all this? What equivalent am I expected to give you for so liberal a compensation?"

His face took a look of amaze at this question.

"Is it possible," he inquired, "that you still misunderstand my meaning? But surely you must comprehend me; and to prove to you — if your doubt lies in that direction — that I actually mean business, I hereby beg leave to deposit with you five hundred dollars with which to make yourself and family comfortable until "——

Quick as a flash the truant senses returned to our heroine, and with them furious indignation. As he laid the notes on her lap — they were new notes, beautiful, fresh, and tempting! — she took them between her fingers and twisted them until they came apart, then throwing them, in a storm of scorn and anger upon the floor, said, —

"I have put my children to bed hungry to-night, sir, and have scarcely tasted food for two days myself, and as far as the body is concerned am ready to perish. There lies the money with which you would tempt me to earn the wages of sin and shame! Take it, and with it the recollection that you have met one woman who would a million times rather starve herself, and see her children drop dead at her feet, than become the victim of any man's lust. Take it, and leave my house this instant, and never dare show your villainous face to me again."

Utterly crestfallen, he stooped to pick up the torn notes, and then, turning on his heel, without a word complied with her emphatic invitation, even to the last clause, for she never did see his face again. A day or two after, however, came a grocer's wagon to her door, with a supply of provisions sufficient to last for a considerable time ; and, though no name was sent with them, she felt sure that this man was the donor. The City Hall clock pealed out the hour of nine as her visitor departed. She closed the doors, and then looked her situation full in the face again. Had God quite forsaken her ? she asked herself. Had the good angels forgotten all about herself and dear ones? Something must be done. The babies had sobbed themselves to sleep. Teardrops still glistened on little Josey's cheek. She was so faint herself from long fasting that she could with difficulty lift baby, who refused to be comforted without another attempt to draw sustenance from the fount which never before had so entirely failed her. Her duty was now plain. The probabilities were, if she waited until morning before an effort was made to procure food she would be too ill to take further care of her family. So, with the moaning infant in her arms, she knocked at the door of a neighbor's house. Even then pride was mighty. How could she tell a human soul of her starving condition? What though the neighbor was a friend — one who had always appeared interested in everything concerning her — this was begging, nothing else. As she stood waiting for the door to open memory went back to the funeral sermon preached at the burial of her father, when the minister had declared that the seed of the righteous should never be forsaken, and yet here she was begging bread. What wonder, then, that the poor woman doubted that such a thing as justice ever existed; that she questioned all goodness and mercy, and asked herself, as millions have before, what possible good such wretchedness could accomplish. The door was opened by the lady herself.

"Why, my dear," she inquired, "what is the matter? You are as pale as death; and the baby, too, out at this time of night! Why, child, what has happened? Has he got home?"

Not a man, woman, or child in the neighborhood but detested the man our friend called husband, and the neighbors naturally concluded that this might probably account for her haggard appearance and evident distress.

"No; I have not heard a word from that quarter," replied Nellie; "but my children are starving, and I am so weak from continued fasting that I can hardly stand. For Heaven's sake attend to us quickly, or we shall die!"

"Oh! how could you?" cried the neighbor. "My dear, how could you suffer so without telling me? You know I love you as one of my own children."

If there happen to be any among my readers who know from experience what hunger is, they can appreciate the feelings of our friend, when she re-entered her own house supplied with an ample supper for her children. The two older ones were lying awake, — growing boys with healthy appetites, who had gone supperless to bed after a day of scanty fare. Little Josey, whose patient suffering had so pierced his mother's heart, when plaintively asking God for "some more milk," was waked from the sobbing sleep he had fallen into, and fed, as were all the rest, with good, nourishing food. Starvation was once more warded off. Now what should she do? She could not subsist on charity. "I will try and write something," she murmured softly to herself. "Who knows but I may succeed. Surely every avenue of honorable employment cannot be closed against me." All alone, in the still hours of night, by the light of a solitary flickering candle, she commenced her work. Eleven — twelve — one — two — three o'clock sounded out on the calm night, and still she wrote. No sound was heard save the steady scratching of the pen, and the breathing of the sleeping little ones, which latter sound seemed to spur her more earnestly on. As a lover of music marches animatedly and in good time to the strains of martial melody, so did this anxious, earnest mother write to the music of her children's breathing. Four o'clock, and the manuscript was finished. Trembling with mingled hope and fear she read it carefully through, and then, tying it lovingly up with a piece of blue ribbon, laid it away and retired. The morning light found her dubious and almost hopeless. She was aware how hard it was for one not possessed of any literary reputation to sell anything. Nowhere as much as in the literary world does the vulgar old saying hold good, "Get your name up, and you can lie in bed till noon." Equally applicable is the French proverb, *C'est le premier pas qui coute.* But she could not afford to be daunted by considerations like these. However forlorn the hope might be, it had the flavor of hope still, and her children must have bread. With a tremor in her heart, and yearning in her "scherin" eyes that doubtless had the force of a plea with the kind editor to whom she offered her story, she waited for his reply.

"A story I see?" said he, after a casual examination, folding it up again.

"Can you not read or have it read now?" she inquired. "I would so like to know about it."

"Doubtless," he answered. "But I am just going away for the day, and shall not have a moment until to-morrow morning; but let me tell you one thing, my dear woman, do not for mercy's sake be too hopeful in regard to its acceptance. We are completely overrun with stories of this description. You have written before, I presume, and know all about these things."

"No, sir," she moaned, trembling with the expected disappointment. "This is my first attempt."

"Well, well, child," he interrupted, kindly, almost paternally; "do not borrow any trouble about it. Probably if it doesn't answer for us, it may for some one else. Come in to-morrow about this hour, and I will tell you all about it."

None but those who have been through this

trying ordeal of waiting can understand Nellie's feelings through the remainder of the day. She went on time the next morning, though, you may believe. The editor met her with a kind smile, and the manuscript in his hand. It had lost its blue ribbon, and it seemed to her invested with a new charm since its lodgment in the editor's desk.

"Well!" said he, smiling; "what do you think about it?"

"Oh, I don't know," replied his visitor, vainly trying to control herself.

"It is wicked," said he, "to keep you on the anxious-seat so long, my child. I have taken your story: it is a very good one, and there is nothing to hinder your making a good long mark in the world of letters. Here is your check; you can get it cashed at the desk."

Desks, chairs, inkstands, papers, books, assistant-editors, and proof-readers went bobbing round for a moment in strange confusion. It required a pretty strong will-power to keep from fainting just then; but, as in previous instances, will conquered, and Nellie presented herself at the desk for her money, received the astonishing sum of thirty-five dollars, and went on her way rejoicing. There was not a prouder or happier woman in America than was she, as she pressed her precious darlings to her bosom, knowing that now she possessed the means within herself to ward off hunger from her little ones. Here, then, was proof that money was to be earned by story-writing. This door had not shut in her face, but had opened with frank promise and welcome. She was encouraged and happy. There were bread, clothing, and shelter for her dear ones within easy and honorable reach. She went on writing, with more or less success, until she had secured a welcome for her articles in several of the literary papers of the city. But now the chord, which had been stretched beyond its strength, threatened to break. It often happens so. While the full tension is on, the slender thread seems strong; slacken it, and it shows how little there is left of it. It was so with our friend's physical energy. Her overtaxed brain and nervous system revenged themselves the moment they had opportunity to do so. Brain

fever supervened. For weeks the poor child lay
helpless and **suffering,** happily unconscious however, a part of the time, that she was no longer
able to support her children. During this long
struggle **for** the necessaries of life, **our** friend
had had ample opportunity to test friendship.
In a few instances she had found the precious
gem, **and** finding, had valued **and** enjoyed it as
every true woman must. She had waded
through deep waters, had been subjected **to** per-
secution and misconstruction, had added practice
to her natural discrimination, and had come to
judge accurately between the specious and the
real, the false and the true. Now she was ill,
and unable to provide for her family; and God,
who never **utterly** forsakes his little ones, sent a
friend to her relief. That friend was a man,
and that man, strange **as** it may seem here, a
Broad street broker, who, notwithstanding the
din, bustle, and excitement consequent upon the
rise and fall of stocks, had both time and disposition to assist those in need of assistance.
There was no love in the premises, save that
tender and unselfish brotherly affection which

every true man must feel for a delicate woman battling with the dreadful realities of life.

When friendship *does* exist between a man and woman, the links are wonderfully strong. For weeks this friend ministered to the invalid, providing for every want, and assuming the whole responsibility of the family. No matter who he is; you will find him any day in Broad street; but his name is known to the angel who wrote "Ben Adhem" as "one who loved his fellow-men." Convalescence from this illness was slow but sure, and Nellie again found herself able to use her pen. With no regular salary, dependent entirely upon the sale of the articles she was compelled to grind out each week, it was of course terribly up-hill work; and then, too, she found herself compelled to fight for every inch of the ground she travelled. And now another word upon the misconstruction to which pure and delicate-minded, yet natural and impetuous women are constantly subjected in their struggle for success in the business of life. The story of the pretty French girl, as told in "Packard's Monthly," raised a curious cry of op-

16

position from the smaller fry of the press. "It was ridiculous," they declared. "Very clearly impossible!" "No editor, or respectable man of any profession, would ever insult and take advantage of a young woman in that way, if her own conduct did not furnish him an invitation to do so. Thousands of women," they persisted, "went daily in and out of newspaper offices, transacting their business with as much freedom as men, and were treated, in fact, with more respect and deference than men could be." In the majority of instances this is undoubtedly the case. It is no part of our purpose to slander the profession of literature in the person of the *preux chevaliers* who have adopted it. And yet not only is the French girl's story true, but many another like it might be told by women whose very unconsciousness of evil has led them to treat the *betes noirs* of the profession with a naturalness and spontaneity of manner that such natures can never understand. The idea that the treatment women receive at the hands of men depends exclusively on their own deportment is also encouraged by some women. Not

long ago I had the pleasure of listening to a conversation between a well-known dramatist and
litterateur, and an equally well-known poetess of
New York City.

Said the former: "I see no need of women
raising this outcry in regard to insult. For my
part, I have never met with any such trouble.
I can always command respect, because I am
always myself, and know how to assert myself.
Misconstruction? Heigho! That is all nonsense."

"In your case perhaps it is," replied her
witty companion, flushing crimson to the very
roots of her hair. "There are those, most certainly, whom the obtusest of the obtuse could
not in any manner misconstrue. They invite
freedom and receive it—make no fuss about
it, because it is the diet they are accustomed
to; and these are the very women who cry out
the loudest against their own sex. These are
the women who make men bad, and keep them
bad. My experience has been not at all like
yours. I have self-respect, but have not found
that my mere presence was always a sufficient

assertion of it. In fact," doubling up her little hand and extending it towards her interlocutor, " I have on two or three occasions in my life, as a writer, been obliged to aid the logic of that presence with the more irresistible and comprehensible logic of this fist."

These are hard facts, but facts nevertheless. Sometimes I have reasoned with myself after this wise: This dreadful condition of things is consequent upon the violation of some law. At a fire at sea, in a gale of wind, or any extraordinary occurrence where the courage and good behavior of men need to be exhibited, it often happens that they fall far short of the manly, to say nothing of the heroic work. Conflagrations and earthquakes are out of the natural order of things; and so, it seems to me, is the war which women are compelled to wage for their bread and butter; and this may account for the strange conduct of some business men towards women compelled to labor. It is not what they have been taught to consider the original plan, and so they fail to appreciate the motives which drive women into counting-rooms and printing-offices.

To me there is something terribly out of joint in
the idea of a woman's hand-to-hand tussle with
business. It seems quite enough for women to
bear the children of the world, and educate them
for positions of trust and responsibility; and the
mother of a family will find but little time for
business details if she attend carefully and conscientiously to her household. Wifehood and
motherhood will not prevent literary pursuits.
On the contrary, women who write because they
love to write, and on this account cannot help
writing, invariably write well. In **fact, as** every
human being, man or woman, instinctively feels,
there is something about woman **that** utterly
unfits her for this rough-and-tumble life. It
seems to me that God could never have intended
that she should be the bread-winner. Her minis-
try is not in the outer courts of the temple, but
belongs rather to the Holy of the Holies. We
speak here of things as they ought to be, not as
they are. Woman's best **right, after all** is said
and done, is the right to a good husband; and
the truer this doctrine is, the more it will be ap-
parent to every acute mind **that** she can be con-

tent with nothing short of that consummation. With a half-way good husband she has only half her rights, and with a bad one she is in the condition of an utter slave. Knowing that she has the natural right to a protecter and provider, if, in order to secure moral and physical safety to herself and her children, she finds it necessary to leave the man whose name she bears, must she not find the struggle for bread unnatural and repugnant, and must she not become unnerved, shattered, rasped — ready in any moments of anguish to lie down and die from sheer exhaustion and discouragement? There are, of course, some women who possess to a certain degree masculine traits; but we are speaking only of those whose womanhood is most perfect. I will venture to say that there cannot be found one woman in ten who earns her living away from home and home loves, who will say that such a life is desirable. I have talked with hosts of them.

"My dear," I have said to more than one poor struggling soul, "what of all things here below would you most prefer, provided your wish could be granted?"

The invariable answer is, while tears will fill the tired eyes: "Oh, somebody to love me and take care of me."

Mark well, oh ye who declare that woman's happiness can be complete without conjugal love—THAT SOMEBODY IS NEVER A WOMAN. This comes from no desire to shirk work, but because they feel the utter uncongeniality of their employment.

Notwithstanding all this, the dreadful knowledge stares us in the face that woman must labor—must, like her brother, earn her living by the sweat of her brow. There is no way of evading it. Would to God there were! and that they could fill the positions which, from the duties expected of them, they seem best fitted for. Would that every true woman's heart could be filled to the brim with good, honest love. What a glorious world this would be to live in then! Now, while I conscientiously believe that every woman pushed into the world to toil in the same pursuits as man (I say nothing of the hun-

dred in every thousand who enjoy such elbow-
ing) is really out of her sphere. I realize also
that this cannot be prevented, and that protection
by law is the just due of such. If women must
work, and in order to accomplish a given result,
must labor twice as assiduously as their brothers,
then surely there is no justice in any law which
deprives them of a single one of their rights.

Up to this time our friend had never seen Miss
Anthony—that earnest, ardent, and most devoted
champion of woman's political rights. She had
become greatly interested in her manner of put-
ting things, although unable to believe, as does
this good woman, that men and women stand
upon the same intellectual platform. She had
noticed that girls with the same advantages, educational and other, as boys, spent a large part of
their leisure time playing with dolls, and talking
to the minature representations of the beauty and
splendor of their mythical "papa;" that while
boys sometimes stopped from their game of ball
or tag to tap a pretty girl under the chin, or
mend her hoop, they would again resume the
game, utterly oblivious that said little girl, very

likely, stood in the same spot expecting another similar demonstration. She had also seen that in anything requiring severe analytical study, boys were, as the rule, ahead, while in music, composition, rhetoric and the like, girls were quite up to the mark; and realized from this general and especial observation that women, if they live at all as they desire, must live in the affectional, and that women by nature are more tender and considerate than men.

Our friend finally concluded to call upon this defender of women, Miss Susan B. Anthony, and judge for herself of her characteristics.

Miss Anthony was engaged, but would be at liberty presently. So, with a natural feeling of awe, Nellie seated herself to wait. Imagination pictured a loud-voiced, unprepossessing Abigail of masculine proportions and warlike demeanor, whose hands were fists and whose feet extended themselves involuntarily whenever a man approached; so that when the door of an inner office opened, and a pleasant-faced womanly woman appeared, she cast down her eyes again and prepared to wait a little longer. A pair of eye-glasses were raised to the mild, gray orbs, our friend surveyed for a moment doubtingly (Miss A. has not the happy faculty of remembering faces), and then, while a friendly smile lit up her features, Susan advanced to where the stranger sat.

"Did you wish to see me, madam?" she inquired hastily, and with a preoccupied air. Evidently the "Revolution" was behind time.

"I am waiting for Miss Anthony," replied Nellie.

"Well, I am that individual," she answered. "You have probably seen some newspaper description of me, and so failed to recognize. You must never form your opinion of any public character by report, cartoon, or editorial. They don't treat us well at all. But what is the matter with you? You look as though you had been crying steadily for the last six months."

Nellie smiled a little sadly, but said nothing. The revolutionary veteran continued: "Now, my dear woman, this is all wrong. Women never will accomplish anything until they stop crying.

I don't know why it is, but they seem to consider tears a badge of honor, and their duty, as well as privilege, to boo-hoo on all occasions. Men never cry! Just imagine a man sitting down and weeping because some little screw in his life-machinery is loose. Do you think if he did a man would stop to help him fix it? No, indeed! I tell you, with less brine there would be more common-sense exhibited."

"Yes, Miss Anthony, very true," replied our friend. "But some women have great excuse for tears: I have had."

"Great cause for sorrow, no doubt; but until women learn to restrain emotion they will always be in the condition of slaves. If a woman is unhappy in her domestic ralations, crying doesn't help it. On the contrary, it ruins her eyesight, breaks her constitution, causing her to grow prematurely old; and when the time comes for that woman to go out into the world and scratch for herself and children, as many are compelled to, it finds her shattered and unnerved, in no condition to stand up and fight for her rights, as they all have to when brought into competition with men of business. You are earning your own living, I suppose?"

"Yes, madam; my own living and that of my children."

"I thought so," she replied. "The same old story. I wish it was in my power to help substantially the hosts of suffering women I am thrown in contact with every day of my life, but all I can say is, do the best you can. By and by, the ballot will straighten out things. Take my advice, now: don't let fall another tear!"

This was but the first of many very pleasant interviews that our friend enjoyed with Susan B. Anthony. Here, too, she became acquainted with Mrs. Stanton, that genial, lovable person whom all admire, even though they may differ seriously from her in opinion. The sight of these two women working together for the same great cause sufficiently illustrates the difference between unison and harmony. Miss Anthony, intensely energetic and abstracted, pleads for her sex from a point beyond mere feminine sympathy; while Mrs. Stanton is all woman, and every word she speaks comes out of a heart conscious of its needs as a woman, while in her own person she is an exemplification of true wifehood and motherhood. From her our friend always felt sure of winning that full measure of sympathy and appreciation, that toleration of female weakness and heart-want, which the masses strangely enough consider prominent women incapable of understanding.

Up to this time not a single word had been heard from the unnatural husband and father. He might be dead his relatives argued; but Nellie, although willing to place the most favorable construction possible on his silence and absence, felt confident that he was alive, and that he would be sure at some future time to pounce down upon her, disturbing the peace and independence so recently found. She tried to convince herself she was no longer his wife; that his brutal conduct and subsequent desertion had effectually divorced her; but there was the terrible legality of the marriage staring her in the face. In her agony lest he might at any time return, and, acting upon her refusal to live with him again as his wife, snatch the children from her, she consulted an eminent New-York lawyer to see what action had best be taken in the premises.

The honorable gentleman heard her through, and then remarked, while his face flushed with indignation, —

"It is a cruel shame that a divorce cannot be granted in this eminently virtuous State for the causes you describe; but unless you can prove that scamp guilty of adultery I can do nothing for you, except to assist you in procuring a separation — *a mensa et thoro* — which, as a friend, I would advise you not to apply for. If wary and patient, you may succeed in procuring a divorce, *a vinculo.*" And then followed advice in reference to watching the individual, and if not successful in such espionage, to finding some one capable of luring him into the haunts of vice, from which counsel our friend recoiled in horror, as must every honest, high-minded woman.

The days wore on. A year flew rapidly by. On account of her inability to furnish her apartments as her position now demanded, and having, with the incessant labor of her new profession, little time for the details of housekeeping, Nellie procured board for herself and family, and gave her attention exclusively to literature.

One day, while busily engaged in her work, a servant entered, and informed her that a gentleman awaited her in the parlor.

"What name did he give?" inquired Nellie.

"Oh, none, ma'am," replied the waitress. "Sure and I asked him; but he said 'twas no matter; you'd know when you got there."

She sprang to her feet with a sudden conviction. It was her "clog" returned to annoy her. No other man would ever have sent so insulting a message. She opened the parlor door, pale and trembling. Sure enough, there he sat, coolly ensconced in the corner of a sofa. As though he had parted from her but yesterday, he arose, extended his hand, saying, while a devilish smile played around his mouth, —

"How are you, duckey? You look as pretty as a pink!"

"I am very well, sir," she responded, stiffly. "But to what unforseen circumstance am I indebted for this visit?"

"Nonsense, Nellie! Don't go to getting sarcastic, for you know I never could stand that! and don't get excited about tifles. Why, I declare, you have grown fleshy, and pretty too! You've a nice snug place here. Been boarding long?"

"About six months," she replied.

"What did you give up housekeeping for?" was the next query.

"Because, after your sale and destruction of household articles, I had nothing to keep house with."

"Where are the children? I expect the baby has grown to be quite a girl."

The two youngest were called, and after being taken on his knee for a single moment, were dismissed with the remark, —

"Now run away; I want to talk to mamma."

No sooner had they gone than he turned to Nellie, and with a proprietor's air, said, —

"Where is our room, duckey? I am as tired as the ———."

"Our room! *My* room is upstairs, sir!" she answered, with bursting indignation. "You have no place in *this* house, and never will have in any house that I occupy. I have done with you forever."

"Done with me forever? That's a rich joke!" and the wretch burst into a paroxysm of laughter. "Why, the little woman has been a widow so long, she really believes she is her own mistress. Have you quite forgotten, then, that we stood up before a minister, once on a time, and you promised to love, honor, and obey — to take for better or for worse, until death did us part — this individual who stands before **you**? Ay! duckey, I have got you now! Come, no more airs. Show a fellow where you live. Upon my word, you haven't the slightest idea how tired I am."

"Neither do I care, sir," and the slight form was straightened to its utmost dignity. "And have the kindness to leave the house immediately. I am supporting myself and children, and especially request that you will in the future, as you have in the past year, let me and mine alone. I promise that you shall never be annoyed by me, under any circumstances, except,

17

indeed, it be in the matter of divorce, which I intend at some time to procure."

Checkmated! That he thoroughly realized. For a moment he stood as if petrified; then his rage burst forth in a perfect volley of curses.

"Well!" he exclaimed, "if you try that game, I'll take every ———— young one you've got away from you! I wonder how my lady will relish that?"

"Take them if you can!" replied the intense little woman. "Notwithstanding, I am your legal wife, and you are the legal father of these children, I do not believe there can be found a court of justice, in the length and breadth of the land, that would give you the custody of them. Might makes right, in almost every instance, and I have proved myself capable of taking care of them — which you never have! and I shouldn't be afraid to trust the decision of any so-called honorable body. So try it, and I will fight you to the last gasp, and keep my children too."

A few moments after our *ci-devant* lord and master left the house, having been afforded a fine opportunity for reflection. He was now, as may be imagined, at his wits' ends! Out of business, out of clothes, penniless, and determined not to work unless the employment exactly suited his fastidious taste,—the gentleman was sadly in need of a home, and a wife to support him, which, strange to relate, our friend couldn't be made to feel her duty For some time he kept exceedingly quiet, annoying her only by letters, in each of which he expressed his penitence for past misdeeds eloquently imploring mercy, in no instance forgetting to state that he was entirely out of money; to all of which appeals she turned a deaf ear. For " conduct "unbecoming a mason," he had been expelled from his lodge, and now sought favor again in he eyes of his brethern. By means of tears, and promises of reform, he worked upon their manly sympathy to the extent of persuading them to act as his ambassadors. Upon no account would our friend be tempted into saying or thinking an unkind thought of the fraternity of which he was once an honored member. Notwithstanding his expulsion, many of the members of the lodge personally sympathized with and aided her by advice, promises of protection, and in one or two instances, pecuniarily. They could not tolerate him in their society; she could not live with him as her husband: so far the lodge and herself were in sympathy. Committees of masons were appointed to visit her, and endeavor to induce her to welcome the prodigal. On one of these occasions, after having explained to her their ideas of the duties of the case, and laid before her, in eloquent terms, the immense responsibility devolving upon her as a wife and mother, she made answer,—

"Gentleman, as God lives, I have faithfully performed my part of the marriage contract. Because I was a wife, and believed in the sacredness of my wifely compact, I bore patiently every description of abuse possible to conceive of — torture so terrible, gentlemen, that words would **fail** to describe it. Desertion he then added to the list of horrors, and for one year was not heard from. During a portion of that year my children have been hungry and cold, suffering for the commonest necessaries of life. Through the keenest physical and mental anguish, by God's help and my own determination, I have conquered circumstances, and find myself thoroughly competent to support my little family; and now, having reached this satisfactory position, you ask me to take again to my bosom a man who has never been to me anything but a brute,— a man who left his wife and children to starve and die. Have you restored him to full fellowship in your lodge ?"

"Oh, no!" one of them replied. "Such an action would be in direct disobedience to the rules of our order. It is possible he may be reinstated at some future time,— at least we hope so. It depends entirely upon his subsequent conduct. The cases are not analogous at all."

"Perhaps not," replied Nellie; "but it amounts to just this: You naturally distrust his protestations of reform, and find yourselves unable and unwilling to restore him to the privileges of your order; but you would fain convince me that it is my duty to bring this man into the most intimate and sacred of human relations. Gentlemen, I fail to see the logic of your argument."

After this last turning of the tables, as may be imagined, there were no more committees of masons appointed to visit her. Failing to accomplish his purpose by this means, he suddenly fell to making professions of religion, and thus enlisted the sympathies of prominent ministers of the gospel—every one of whom Nellie in turn resisted.

"Your husband appears very fond of you," said one of those divines, "and seems to dote on his children."

"Yes," replied Nellie, a little sarcastically, it must be confessed,—"his past conduct has fully demonstrated the depth and intensity of his affection for both wife and children."

"But, my friend, can you not allow bygones to be bygones? Can you not, for the sake of future happiness, forgive and forget?"

"That is precisely what I am trying to do, if his friends will only allow me. I can bury the man, and his misdeeds, beyond all possibility of resurrection."

"But, madam, you are his wife,—his wife in the sight of God."

"*That*, sir, I deny. To my shame, I am obliged to confess myself his legal partner ; but, in God's sight I am no more his wife than I am yours, nor so much,—for between us there may be some bond of sympathy."

As may be inferred, the parson was somewhat shocked, and entered his most solemn protest.

" Do not, I beseech you, my dear madam, allow yourself to be inoculated with the loose ideas at present prevailing in reference to marriage. The past has probably been bitter; but it is a wife's duty to forgive everything, and to be ready to believe anything. You should remember your sacred promise — keep it constantly before you — to love, honor, and obey until death."

" Sir," said Nellie, " you know nothing whatever of this man ; nothing of me, except what he has chosen to represent. You have come armed with all the panoply of your profession, eloquent with texts of scripture, wrested to suit my peculiar case; but all this can make no impression upon me. My heart has cicatrized at last, and can no longer feel any sense of especial duty towards the man whose cause you are pleading, unless indeed it be the duty I owe myself and children of letting him gloriously alone. My dear sir, I would have you answer me one question. What *is* a wife? Taking you on your probable answer that it is a woman who has publicly promised to love, honor, and obey a man until death should part them twain, — I would again ask, Can a woman keep this promise unconditionally? Are love and honor and obedience still **due** a man who has himself violated every promise of his own; who abuses, contaminates, insults, fails to provide for, and finally forsakes the woman he has promised to love and cherish? and is marriage then a mere physical **bond** perfectly consistent with hatred and disgust? Am I the wife of that man? Has not every law of right already divorced us; and would not any sanction the law might give to such divorce be a mere form — the mere opening of a wooden door? So it seems to me, sir; and all the argument that the combined force of all creation could bring to bear on this subject would not move me a hair's-breath."

"Then, I suppose, it is no use for me to say

any more; but I do beseech of you to be careful.
You are still young and comely—love may be
offered you, Mrs. ——. I have no doubt but it
will be so. Oh, madam, I shudder to think of
it!" and the agitated parson wrung his hands in
bitterness of spirit.

"If love is offered me,—real, genuine love,"
replied Nellie, who could with difficulty suppress
a roar, "I have an indistinct sort of an idea that
I shall accept it, and be wonderfully thankful
therefor. Love, you know, to use your own
weapons (scripture weapons), is but 'a fulfilling
of the law ;' 'love worketh no ill to its neighbor,'
etc. I should be basely forgetful of first principles did I reject the inestimable gift. I have
never yet loved,—never seen the man to whom
my heart can bow down in homage, saying, 'You
are my conqueror.' Four years of practical wid-
owhood, during which the most intense stretch
of every faculty has been an every-day experi-
rience, during which, day by day, and week by
week, the cry of my children for bread must be
met and answered, left me but little time to think
either of what 'might have been,' or 'might yet

be;' and yet I possess a woman's dearest needs and intensest yearnings. I believe, with Miss Diana Mulock,—that most conservative of conservatives, who, like all poets, speak the truth in spite of themselves, that —

> ' Duty's a slave that holds the keys,
> But love, the master, goes in and out
> Of his goodly chambers, with song and shout —
> Just as he please — just as he please.' "

It is needless to say that after this the clergyman took his leave.

To this day our friend has remained firm in her determination. Living with her all these years of struggle and heart-ache opened my soul to the terrible woes which a large class of women endure at the hands of the law, and gave me strength and courage to cry out with all my woman's might against its terrible injustice. At this time, when my head was bowed almost to the earth with affliction, the heroine of " Up Broadway" was strangely thrown in my path, and with her consent, and that of her husband, I determined to give the story to the world.

There is another thing which it will be well

to take into consideration before leaving this subject. Woman, whether made to be loved or not, no one will deny is made to love. One of the arguments used by men against her occupying certain places requiring intellectual strength, is that she is made to live in the affections. So she is. The woman who becomes too sorrowful, or too hardened by any experience, to love, is wanting in the distinctive womanly attributes given her by God. Suppose now the deluded, cheated, abused, disgusted wife, whose nature is none the less loving because of her sorrow, and certainly needing love all the more, meets some man who would be to her, strength and happiness; and suppose they mutually love. Such things have been. Is she for what was her dire misfortune to be doubly punished, and doomed to be legally bound to the man who has kept not one of the vows of his marriage bond? Is it just that his cruelty, drunkenness, or desertion should go for nothing in the eye of the law, and she be obliged to have his secret footsteps dogged to prove him adulterous? Or suppose another case: A good man has a termagant

wife : his home is made wretched with her vixen-
ish disposition, till he is glad to seek refuge from
her sight in club, lodge, or bar-room. Even the
gambler's hell is often less infernal than a man's
house. Why should he, in order to be legally
free from the thorn in his side, be able not only
to 'prove her unbearable in temper, but unclean
in morals? The law will grant a separation;
why, then, not a divorce? Will you answer
because the law of God says for this cause (adultery) alone? Do you pretend that the divorce
law of the State of New York is founded on
divine law? Where, then, do you find in Holy
Writ, that an offence which sends a man to
State's prison is adulterous? but that is legal
ground for divorce. Where do you find that
desertion for **seven years** is adulterous? yet that
is also legal ground for divorce. Does **it** not
seem that these laws of a State made by *men*,
were fashioned by them to suit their own conscience, and then salted a little with scripture to
season them? Do not **say it** is as hard upon man
as woman. It is not so. A man may leave his
loving or unloving spouse, and so long as he does

not *openly* outrage any of the social proprieties, no disgrace attaches to him. Let a woman leave the man who maltreats her, and in nine cases out of ten, she must henceforth walk more than widowed. At once she is regarded with suspicion. The widow may enter freely into society, but the deserting or the deserted wife, whether in the house or by the way, must guard every look, word, and action. She is in constant danger, in the most innocent of her actions, of compromising herself. She has no liberties; she never is her "own mistress." Every gossip and scandal-monger has a right to watch and criticize her movements. In many communities a woman is almost as much disgraced by the fact of having parted from her husband, as she would be if she had committed a crime. It is always hard for her to obtain respectable employment. Of course, the better educated and more enlightened the community, the less likely it would be to take this view; but even the best are apt to look with a slight degree of suspicion upon such, and receive her demands for acceptance and appreciation with a grain of social salt. And if she dares accept friendship and sympathy from any man, what an object of interest she at once becomes to Mrs. Grundy!

We would not for the **world that** any change should be made that we **did** not in our heart of hearts believe would be for the best good of society. The outcry that **has** of late been made, of danger **to** public morals, as the result of any change in the strictest marriage laws, is in our opinion **quite** gratuitous. Don Quixote **will** always be ready to fight wind-mills; but the free winds of heaven will not be constrained by the arm of any old fogy, whether individual or collective. We do not believe that any permanent **evil** could possibly result from an amelioration of **the laws of divorce,** as they exist on the statute-books **of the** State of **New York.** Is Connecticut any **less** moral than other States? and yet the divorce laws there are **far** less rigid than those of any Eastern State; exceeded **in** liberality by none in **the** Union, except those **of** Indiana. Of course, in both these States, there are **more** divorces than in any others, and why? Simply because the laws of other States are so rigid as to induce many outsiders to flock thither: just as the Southern slaves used to flee to Canada for freedom. Since the emancipation of slavery that hegira has stopped; and so would the hegira of men and women to Indiana in search of freedom from hateful marriage bonds, if the laws of other states were framed upon the liberal principles which govern these. Out of the abundance of the heart the author has written the preceding pages. That they may arouse good men and women to the injustice so potent to all who will think, is her fervent desire. God grant it!

THE END.